PENNGROVE PONDEROSA

PENNGROVE PONDEROSA

Surviving the Social and Sexual Revolution of the 1970s in Northern California

A Novel

Nathaniel Robert Winters

2014 Buffalo Printing Company Trade Edition

A special thanks to Alyson Hitt, Chris Lameda, Kathleen Patterson, Carol Troy and Mary O'Leary.

BUFFALO PRINTING COMPANY
Napa Valley California

Dedicated to three special Bands of Brothers

My fellow Vietnam Veterans and the people in the United States who worked to bring us home and end the war.

My fellow teachers who fight the good fight in the classrooms of our country. Their dedication inspired me every day.

A group of Sonoma State students in the seventies who nicknamed themselves RAGs. Thanks for letting this history buff crash your party.

Chapter 1
California or Busted

The sun glowed golden on the horizon as they drove
west toward that bright ball in the late summer
Nebraska evening. Corn was everywhere, swallowing
the car like the whale that consumed Jonah. They
could not see anything through the twelve-foot-high
crop except the lined blacktop of the straight
unending road reaching to the sunset. Don Goldman

and John Booth were cruising through the mid-
western American countryside on a mission, to get to
Treasure Island before Bill's ship came in.
Meanwhile, they savored the experience of the cross
country trip to California.

Ahead of schedule, the two boys didn't have
to hurry. So they left the interstate to drive on the old
two lane state highway, sunglasses wrapped around
their faces providing a protection against the sun-
drenched glare. Don drove his car, a 1968 Mercury
Cougar, the one with the mod turn signal that didn't
just blink on and off like all other cars. Four lights
would glow in sequence in the direction the car was
turning, making the Mercury unique and very cool, an
instant classic.

Childhood friends, Don and John Wilkes were
not just going to California, but to San Francisco, the
1972 home of the counterculture, antiwar protest, and
hippies. Also it was home to their mission's
destination, Treasure Island Naval Base on an island
in the middle of San Francisco Bay. Bill Silver,
childhood buddy, was being discharged from the

Navy after a tour in Vietnam. His ship was due to arrive in just a few days.

John Booth was a happy co-pilot. Everybody called him Wilkes, even though that wasn't his middle name. His parents failed to realize that by naming him Jonathan it would remind others of the historical assassin, John Wilkes Booth. But Wilkes liked his nickname and had fun with it. As a young boy, whenever anyone teased him, he would make an imaginary gun with his fingers, smile, point and shoot them in the head, then blow as if smoke were coming from his index finger. That would either shut up his protagonist or enrage him enough to chase Wilkes around the schoolyard. Fast, Wilkes was too quick to catch.

Wilkes and Don grew up on Long Island, suburban New York. Their friend Bill was just one of the guys, always playing ball at the school yard then hanging out together through high school.

Don was more quiet and thoughtful than Wilkes. Only five-feet-five tall, he had a beautiful five-foot-eleven-inch sister, Laura, who left most of his high school buddies transfixed.

The two twenty-one year old men avoided the draft with high lottery numbers. Their buddy Bill was not so lucky. He decided to join the Navy before being drafted. His four year enlistment had change to three -- with the Vietnam War winding down, the military was directed to thin out its numbers. Petty Officer William Silver was given the option of a large reenlistment bonus or the early out. When he chose discharge, he was assigned duty to an old destroyer going from Pearl Harbor to San Francisco.

"God, it's flat here, I haven't seen a decent hill since before Cleveland," Wilkes said above the Carlos Santana music blaring from the cassette player.

"Shit!" Don saw the flashing lights of a police car in his rear view mirror. "Wilkes just be cool, don't call him a 'pig' or do anything crazy." Don knew his friend had an outlandish side to him and might get them into trouble. He pulled the car over to the shoulder of the empty road.

"License and registration," the Nebraska highway patrolman said.

"Was I doing anything wrong officer?" Don asked innocently.

The officer was wearing mirrored sunglasses. You couldn't see his eyes. "New York plates, you are a long way from the interstate and a long way from home, aren't you boys? Where are you Yankee-loving guys going?" A big smile was on his face as he handed them back the paperwork.

"We are actually Met fans going to San Francisco, sir," Don replied, trying to seem confident and respectful, worried about the baggy of marijuana in his suitcase in the trunk.

"San Francisco, pervert capital of America," said the uniformed man standing beside the car. He was built solid, looked like he could play linebacker for the University of Nebraska football team.

"We were just looking for a motel to bed down for the night," Wilkes said.

"You boys hippies? Going to San Francisco for a love-in?"

Don said, "Actually were going to pick up a buddy coming home from Vietnam."

The police officer's features softened a little. "Tell you what, the Colorado border is about eighty miles away from here. You boys high-tail it to the interstate and find a motel across the border, out of my jurisdiction, and I won't run you in for failure to get a haircut."

Wilkes temper flared for a second. His ears turned red but he held his tongue.

Don said, "Sure officer, we can do that."

After pulling out onto the road and putting some distance between them and the patrol car, Wilkes shouted, "Oink oink you fucking pig!"

Don added, "Let's get away from these corn huskers. We can be in Denver before midnight."

*

The great Rockies loomed ahead as the road out of Boulder Colorado switch-backed up the mountain. Groves of white-barked aspen trees stood flanked at the side of the road, broad green leaves quaking in the wind. Wilkes put a Creedence

Clearwater Revival cassette into the tape player, his head bobbed while he slapped drums on the dashboard. As they passed the 10,000 foot altitude road sign, the car started to lurch. Don pressed on the gas but the Cougar's, big eight-cylinder engine just sputtered. "Shit, the car was running fine when we left Denver and now the fuckin' engine's is dying."

"Pull over by the turnout, I know what's wrong." Wilkes stopped drumming long enough to point to the side of the road. "It's the carburetor, the air's too thin. I'll get a screwdriver, it's an easy adjustment.

"I knew there was a reason I brought you."

Fifteen minutes later they were back on the road climbing with Creedence blasting from the speakers. As they reached the summit, they pulled the Mercury into a tourist parking spot. A sign showed a map of a short path to Rocky Mountain National Park overlook. The boys, both in good shape, strode up the trail. Don stopped. He became dizzy and had to sit down. Like the carburetor, his brain was not getting enough oxygen in the thin high altitude air.

"Are you all right?"

"Give me a second. I'm a little dizzy." Don could feel his heart racing. He took deep long breaths, put his head between his legs and slowly felt better. "Man that was weird." The two proceeded much slower along the path until they reached the overlook.

The autumn sun was behind them in the late morning, shining a faded glow on the mountain peaks in front of them.

Wilkes said, "I'm thinking of the song lyrics purple mountains majesty, wow."

"Let's go off the trail and smoke that joint in your pocket."

"You sure you feel good enough"?

"I want the opportunity of seeing this highlighted by the ganja."

"Far out man," Wilkes said.

The guys smoked the joint they had rolled earlier until only a roach remained. The boys looked out at an incredible view, highlighted by their altered state. They lay down on their backs and watched as the cumulus clouds formed shapes in the mountain sky.

"That one looks like a mermaid." Wilkes told Don and pointed to the cloud just above them.

"A mermaid, no way dude, what are you smoking" Thinking about what he had just said, Wilkes started laughing. Soon both of them were laughing hysterically.

The clouds grew thicker and darker. All of a sudden they were being hit with drops of rain. By the time they started to retreat down the trail, large drops were coming fast, soaking the boys. Close to the car, rain turned to balls of hail.

"Damn, that hurts!" Wilkes said as he tried to cover his head. As fast as it started, the precipitation ended. The sun peeked out from behind a cloud, almost like Mother Nature was played with the two young men's altered minds.

A large mule deer complete with huge antlers, watched intently as the boys bore down toward him. "Holy shit, look at the size of that deer, have you ever seen a rack that big?" Don asked.

"Not since Judy Zimmerman graduated from

high school," Wilkes giggled.

The two friends froze not knowing if the enormous male might attack. In what was seconds, but seemed much longer, the deer turned and scampered off down the road.

"Man, this must be good pot. What's next a dancing bear?" Wilkes asked. He was wet, cold and shivering in the thin mountain autumn air. The two sat at the edge of the parking lot, the car heater running full blast, smoked another joint and laughed hysterically trying to describe mermaid clouds and the big-racked mule deer.

*

Don and Wilkes spent the night at a small motel. They were back on the road early, bellies full of eggs and pancakes from the local diner. They both flirted with the pretty waitress and invited her to join them on their trip to California. She flirted back, hoping for a big tip but while pouring them another cup of coffee said, "As inviting as that sounds, boys, I don't think my fiancé would like it." She laughed covering her mouth with her hand to hide her crooked teeth in an otherwise beautiful smile. The image and glow of the pretty girl stayed with them as the 68 sports sedan hugged the curves of Colorado State Route 34 headed toward the interstate and then north to Salt Lake City. By evening, they were in the Utah capitol looking for another cheap hotel. The boys found one on the southern outskirts of the city looking at the mountains to the east and the desert to the west. There was a drive-in movie theater just down the street and Don and Wilkes pulled the Cougar into a parking space facing the big screen. Dancing popcorn and Coke bottles preceded the movie *Diamonds are Forever,* with Sean Connery as the suave 007.

Don said, "Remember the time we snuck the girls into the drive-in inside the trunk?"

"Yeah, Lindy and Jody were pissed when we got stuck in that long line, they thought they would never get out. I remember the first time you went out with Lindy, she was so much taller and you had to stand on the front stoop to kiss her goodnight."

"Yeah, but we found a way to deal with all

that by lying down," Don said with a smile, remembering his first sweetheart. "I do miss her, at times. It was sad breaking up when we both went off to college. Last I heard she dropped out of school and joined a commune in upstate New York."

They put the little metal speaker on the driver's side window and rolled it up so they could watch the British spy and Jill St. John defeat Blowfield and save the world again.

*

Don parallel parked in downtown Salt Lake City. In the early morning there was not a cloud in the sky. People hustling to work looked askance at the two long haired tourists walking towards the great temple. Salt Lake City had no cultural divide, suits, white shirts and ties adorned the general public like they were shaped by cookie cutters. The Utah street gave the appearance that the sixties social revolution never occurred. The populous looked like cast of the Ozzie and Harriet 50's TV show, clean-cut and well-tailored. Pop music was not the Rolling Stones, but the Osmonds.

Armed with breakfast in a bag from McDonald's, Don and Wilkes sat across from the temple near the monument to the seagulls that had saved Mormon pioneers from locusts that were devouring their crops a hundred years earlier.

Wilkes said, "I feel like a fish out of water here, maybe seagulls will come and attack me."

"Funny," Don replied as the rising sun warmed him. He unsnapped his jean jacket.

"Don't the Mormons believe we all came from outer space?" Wilkes asked.

"No, that's the Scientologists. The Mormons believe in a prophet from the 1800's named Joseph Smith. He said God spoke to him and became their leader."

"Like the burning bush and Moses? Where was he?"

"Upstate New York," Don answered.

"How do you know so much about the Latter Day Saints?"

"I took a college class on religion."

"Where did the polygamy come in?"

"God told Joseph to have many wives and multiply. So he had more than one wife. You can imagine how the traditional Christians of the 1800's reacted to this group. They ran them out of town and eventually Smith was killed, becoming a martyr. Brigham Young became their leader and brought their wagon trains to Utah."

"So they started out as rebels against traditional religion, with polygamy and leaving the USA to start over, like the hippies. How the heck did they become such conservative Christian patriots?"

"They outlawed polygamy when Utah became a state. They don't drink or smoke so I guess they just evolved to become Nixon Republicans," Don answered.

"Okay," Wilkes said. "Let's get outta here, we can be in Reno tonight and I have just enough green to win our fortune playing blackjack."

*

The salt flats seemed to run forever, north of Interstate 80, so flat and white like God created a road with no borders and no speed limit. The great salt deposit surrounding the Great Salt Lake invited brave or insane dare-devils throughout the twentieth century to try and set land speed records.

"I remember reading about rocket cars out there." Wilkes closed his eyes and imagined rocket-driven racers zooming by like the Ford Cougar was standing still. "Do you want to let this kitty out and see what it can do?"

"That's all right, the road is flat enough, we're going over a hundred. I just hope there are no highway patrol cars around." It appeared the patrolmen had different priorities. Cars flew by, each seeming determined to set their own individual speed record on the horizonless stretch of interstate on that October morning.

"I wonder how the wagon trains survived this endless desert in the summer after crossing the Rockies," Don mused. "Do you realize we drove further in 15 minutes then they could travel in a day?"

"I know, and most of Nevada is desert ahead of us." Wilkes looked out of the window; nothing appeared to grow in the endless salt. He thought about the wagon trains pulled by oxen and mules, heading west like them, looking desperately for water but devoid of gas stations to stop and resupply. "California or bust," he said to Don, with a laugh.

"Yeah, let's not bust or get busted. I can't find any decent radio station. Put on the Eagles tape again. Okay?"

*

The sign said "Welcome to California" and Wilkes immediately inserted the Beach Boy tape he saved for their arrival into the Golden State. The mountain road did not jibe with the beach sound coming from the speakers.

"Truckee, should we get off here and have breakfast?" Don asked. They left Reno at first light, hung over and poorer. Wilkes started out winning at black jack, but the more he drank the worse he played. The casinos knowing all about human behavior, made sure the drinks were free. Don stayed sober and started winning at black jack but lost it all and more in the ten minutes he spent at the craps table.

"Breakfast sounds good, maybe some good black coffee will get rid of my headache," Don said. The car pulled into a diagonal spot on the main street of the mountain town as the Amtrak train to Chicago pulled into the small station just across the street. Sheer granite peaks reached up in front of them beyond the town. They found a dive called the Wagon Wheel Diner and entered a room of western decor.

"This town is not how I pictured California. I guess we are going to have to put off the beach boy lifestyle a little longer," Don said. Yet he was impressed by Truckee's natural beauty.

A slim waitress walked up, brought them a menu and poured them some hot coffee. Wilkes said, "You know what? I think I like this town. There is something unique about it."

The waitress, overhearing their conversation

said, "You should see it here during the ski season, the snow can get ten feet high. We are just fifteen minutes from Squaw Valley."

"You know I never thought of skiing in California. I expected surfboards," Don said.

"There is a lot more to this state than surfboards. That's so LA. Where are you guys coming from?" The cute waitress, with a name tag that said Sally, asked.

"New York," Don replied.

"Oh, that explains it. I'll be right back to get your order." She turned and walked away, hips swaying. The boy's eyes followed the motion.

"I think I'm going to like California." Wilkes said.

They headed out of town after breakfast and stopped at Donner Monument. The boys read about the wagon train that didn't get over the pass before the winter snow that trapped them in 1846. The survivors had to eat the dead to survive.

"They got trapped in late October." Don said, his voice filled with surprise. "What bad luck."

"Maybe we should get over these mountains. Bill comes in tomorrow morning."

*

The U.S.S. Roger Dayton sailed out of thick blinding fog and under the red-tinted Golden Gate Bridge. San Francisco Bay shimmered in the late morning sunshine. The stubborn fog reached out refusing to let go of the Bridge as it retreated back to the cold ocean. As the old destroyer moved into the bay, Bill from his duty station up on the bridge of the ship looked out at a clear sky, revealing the city's skyline. The captain said, "All ahead one third, rudder left 15 degrees." Bill repeated the command into a headphone he wore and the order was repeated in the engine room. The old tin can turned towards Treasure Island. The captain called, "Rudder amidships." The process was then repeated until the ship was tied to the dock. The World War II built destroyer was on its last journey from Pearl Harbor to San Francisco to be decommissioned, back from duty off the coast of Southeast Asia. The ship would join the mothball fleet at the Carquinez Straits, just north of the bay area.

Like the ship, Bill was completing his deployment finishing out his enlistment. He had been ordered to join the old destroyer as the ship's medical corpsman during a fourteen-day uneventful journey from Hawaii to the mainland.

Bill had spent a year with a patrol boat as part of a combined marine and navy squadron as the emergency medical technician on the Mekong River in Vietnam. He had kept many wounded marines and sailors alive until they could be medevac'd out by helicopter but there had been too many he couldn't save including his best friend. The corpsman sick of war, looked forward to his discharge. His papers sat on a desk waiting to be drawn up at the base at Treasure Island.

Don and Wilkes had arrived at the pier earlier and lounged on a railing just back from the dock. Bill spotted them from his sea detail station. He waved and his two high school buddies waved back.

The ship was tied up, the gang plank was lowered and the captain called, "Secure from sea detail."

First Class Petty Officer William Sydney Silver turned to the officer of the deck and said, "Permission to go ashore sir?"

"Permission granted," came the reply. His sea duty completed, Bill saluted the officer and turned to the fantail to give a final salute to the ship's flag.

Bill was wearing his dress white bell bottoms, white short-sleeve top and the traditional white sailor cap. He galloped down the gangplank to embrace his buddies. "God, you two ugly guys look good."

They all laughed, and Don said, "Let's get out of here. San Francisco is waiting."

Chapter 2

Lost and Found in the Bay Area

They parked at North Beach in San Francisco. The three high school buddies sat at a table in a bar just off Broadway, mugs of cold beer in front of them. The calendar on the wall said August 20, 1972. They were catching up, exchanging stories.

After taking a long pull on his mug and wiping the froth from his mouth with the back of his hand, Bill continued, "So I flew from Da Nang to Clark Air Force base in the Philippines, got orders to be on the destroyer at Pearl Harbor and then on to San Francisco. I don't think I've seen a day colder than eighty degrees in over a year. So when we went on sea detail, coming into San Francisco I put on my light cotton dress whites. We were still a few miles out by the Farallon Islands when I went up to the ships bridge to my duty station and of course I couldn't leave. It was so damn cold and windy. The fog was so thick that we had to come in on radar. I was freezing my balls off. I'm talking it felt January, snowy winters cold.

"All of a sudden we were under the Golden Gate Bridge and the sky opened up into the blazing sunshine, I could see all of San Francisco and the whole bay. I can't say I've ever seen a more beautiful sight. I felt warm inside. I might have even wiped a tear from my eye. I hadn't seen the mainland in almost two years.

"You know a friend of mine from the Navy told me that it's really inexpensive to go to college here. I can get the GI bill; might stick around."

Don said, "You know, I have no reason to go back, I might just join you."

Wilkes tried to be the voice of reason. "We just got here. Maybe we should get out of this bar and do some exploring before we plan the rest of our lives. Look at this flyer I got as we came inside." Wilkes showed them a mini poster with incredible artwork of multicolored flowers surrounding a walking skeleton. The poster was for a concert at the Fillmore West featuring the Grateful Dead and two other local bands, medications optional but encouraged.

"Hell yah!" Bill said, "Sounds like fun."

They left the bar and headed for the infamous Haight-Ashbury District. Walking up Haight Street felt like they were exploring a new wonderful country. Hippies openly smoked marijuana on the street.

"I think we're not in Nebraska anymore," Wilkes said to Don and they laughed remembering their experience with that state's highway patrolman.

A tall lanky long haired young man turned to Bill, who was still wearing his uniform, spit on the sidewalk in front of him and said, "So are you one of those Vietnam baby killers?"

Bill, rather than being intimated turned to the confrontational hip-looking guy, smiled and said, "You have no fucking idea, and you don't want to, asswipe." Mr. "Mod" retreated and turned away. Bill rejoined his friends as they gawked at the counter-cultural center of the country.

*

The next morning the fog disappeared from the Bay Area, the weather unusually warm. Young ladies sashayed down Telegraph Avenue in Berkeley clad in short-short or mini-skirts and in the spirit of the women's liberation movement bra-less t-shirts. Young men were dressed in a uniform of cut-off jean shorts and t-shirts. The shirts sported clever political slogans, like the handholding couple walking by: his, "NIXON IS A DICK" and hers, "War Is Not Good for Children or Other Living Things."

The three friends found a coffeeshop-diner

and took their order to the outdoor tables. Bill dressed in civvies, sipped coffee and attacked his first New York style bagel in over a year, complete with cream cheese and lox while Wilkes and Don ate omelets. They soaked the ambiance in of students walking quickly by with books, street vendors putting up art and jewelry, and black men strolling by sporting the popular afro haircut. Bill thought, I want to be part of this.

"The Dead were amazing last night. They kept playing and playing," Wilkes said, between sips of his mocha java. "Did you see all the acid for sale and all the people tripping? The smell of marijuana just permeated the air of the Fillmore, amazing night."

Don asked Wilkes, "Have you ever done acid?"

"No", Wilkes said. "It seems a little too crazy."

"I did it once," Bill confessed.

The other two looked at their buddy with open mouths. "What the hell… when?" Don asked.

"Actually just a few weeks ago." A moment

of silence followed.

"So?" Don asked breaking the quiet.

"I was on leave in Hawaii, waiting for the destroyer to take me to San Francisco. I was staying with an ex-Navy buddy from the Islands. The guy had the best pot smuggled in from Nam. We went snorkeling for the day at Hanama Bay and he asked me if I wanted to do a tab. I thought about it for a few minutes and figured that if I could survive a tour in Vietnam, I could at least survive a day on acid. So I took the tab of window pane."

"So what was it like?" Wilkes asked.

"It was amazing, awesome and scary. The world changed and I became a part of nature, almost on the outside looking in at myself. I felt like I was part of Hanama Bay down to my toes. The beauty and the sunshine were overwhelming. I felt lost in its magnificence.

"My friend Art became my guide. I remember watching a volleyball game on the beach and couldn't figure out how the people could play or keep score. It was all just too complex for my zoned out mind. I remembered asking myself the existential question: Why people would even want to play volley ball?

"I walked over to a palm tree and could see the trunk glowing with energy. I reached out with my hand and could feel the vibrations. I walked down to the water, put my feet in the bay and suddenly felt connected to the rest of the world like my toes were reaching out all the way India, then Africa, then Europe and finally all the way back to Hawaii.

"Art drove me over to the next beach where we body surfed and I felt connected with the sea like I was a dolphin. Then came the sunset and the colors…I just can't describe.

"But as night came, coming down off the stuff was awful. I cried and shook and flashed back to Nam and the Mekong River and the nightmares of that place." Bill shook his head as he finished relating the last sentence.

"Would you do it again?" Don asked.

Bill thought for a second then said, "Maybe…but it would have to be just the right time and place."

The three stayed silent for a few minutes, thinking and taking in the sights of Telegraph Avenue.

Bill asked, "Is New York like this now?"

Don and Wilkes looked at each other. Don shrugged. "Well most of the under 30 crowd dress this way, pretty much, but it's more like downtown San Francisco, some in suits, some hippie looking. Then there's the hip Broadway crowd like the Knicks' Walt Frazier, expensive bell bottoms and hundred dollar wide lapel shirts. You know the look I mean?"

"Yeah," Bill said, "I think so like the new disco dance scene…I hate that, seems so phony, rock music without the musicians." He frowned.

Wilkes nodded in agreement. "You're preaching to the choir. I hate disco."

"I think I may have found us an apartment," Don said changing the subject.

"Where?" Bill asked.

"Not too far from here, the corner of Telegraph and Alcatraz Avenue, just down from the

Co-op market. It's actually an Oakland address not Berkeley."

The boys were pleasantly surprised by the East Bay real estate situation. The New York metropolitan area was divided into ethnic neighborhoods—Irish, Italian, Black, Jewish. When people moved out of the city, they moved into new ethnic neighborhoods in the suburbs. Berkeley and Oakland in the early 70's were amazingly integrated. Money more than skin color decided your place of residence. People with green moved up into the hills.

The three guys took the apartment in the flatland in Oakland, just down from the Berkeley border. Mismatched furniture was found at the thrift store. Neighbors included two University of California Algerian female foreign exchange students on one side and a racially-mixed married couple.

Chapter 3
Tilden Park

Even in uniform, the young woman looked gorgeous, charismatically beautiful. Her dark hair was tied in a ponytail, allowing a full view of the lovely face with a smile that lit up the whole room. She was wearing her dress whites, a second class petty officer in the Navy.

Bill was at Treasure Island Navy Base waiting

patiently for his name to be called for his discharge papers. She grabbed a paper from the stack and called, "WILLIAM SILVER." Bill stood and followed her like a puppy dog watching her hips sway as she walked back to her desk. She turned and their eyes met. He felt a jolt through his whole body.

"I'm Jenny," she said, rolling the paper into her IBM Selectric typewriter. He couldn't take his eyes off her as she typed. She felt his stare and glanced up at his face. She looked him over and smiled. "Well, William after I'm done you will be a civilian. No more dress whites. Too bad they look good on you." She finished typing and took the papers out of the roller. Leaning towards him, her shoulder slightly touching his, she said, "Sign here."

Bill could feel her body against his almost like they were slow dancing. Taking the paper, Jenny pretended to rip up the discharge and giggled. "If I really did that I would have to start over and I could keep you here a little longer."

He took the hint. "How about going out to celebrate with me tonight?" he asked, holding up the discharge and showing her his best smile.

"Can't tonight, I have duty," she said continuing with a southern accent that sounded sexy, like Scarlet O'Hara in *Gone with the Wind*. "But maybe we could do that another time, I think I'd like that."

Bill said, "I heard about a jazz club on the marina at Berkeley. Would you be interested?"

She delayed her answer, acting like she was thinking about it, and then said showing that sweet smile, "I've got a friend, Millie. If you have a friend that will double date, I'll go."

"Can I use your desk phone?"

"Nope, sorry that's only for base calls."

He went out to the hall pay phone, put in a dime and dialed. "Don, how would you like to double date Friday night?"

"With who?"

Bill filled him in on the details and Don said "Okay, but you owe me one, especially if this Millie is a dog."

Bill went back to Jenny's desk. "Okay, my

friend Don says he's on board."

"Well then, you all can pick us up from the gate Friday at twenty-hundred hours."

*

Don drove the Cougar half way across the Bay Bridge, circled around to the base entrance and saw the two young women standing at the gate. Millie was a cute short haired blond with sparkling blue eyes. Bill jumped out of the passenger seat and opened the door for the two ladies. He got in the back with his date.

Jenny looked stunning, her loose hair blowing in the wind. It was the first time he had seen her out of uniform. She was wearing a blue blouse, short skirt which showed off her legs and scarlet high heels. Petty Officer Jenny Brown took Bill's hand into hers, "You know I have a feeling about you. I ran your horoscope and we are quite compatible."

Bill did a Bogart imitation, "This might be the start of a beautiful relationship."

She crinkled up her pretty face and laughed. "Where did that come from?"

"Haven't you ever seen the movie *Casablanca*?"

"Nope, but now I guess I'm going to have to see it."

"Yes, you do. It's one of the classics."

They arrived at the Berkeley marina with a full view of the San Francisco skyline across the bay. The four of them pranced into the Moonlight Jazz and Dinner Club. The lighting in the bar was dark and so were the faces looking at them. They were the only white people in the bar. They stopped in their tracks inside the door. Bill smiled and said, "Come on." He led them to an open table by the bar.

Jenny felt uncomfortable, sat as close to Bill as physically possible, leaned into his ear and said above the music, "Where did you hear about this place?"

Bill smiled, "You're not worried are you? Trust me."

The song ended and the drummer walked up to the table and said, "You honky motherfucker, what are you doing here?"

Bill rose from his seat and hugged the tall black man with a large afro. "Don, Millie, Jenny this is Dave, former Sergeant U.S. Marines."

"This white boy saved my ass." Dave said to the group a little too loudly. People from the other tables overheard and smiled at the new comers.

"Joe, this honky's money is no good, I'm buying," the band member said to the bar tender.

"Not necessary, Dave," Bill said.

"I insist."

When Dave returned to his drums, Jenny turned to Bill and said, "You know how to make a southern girl nervous. If my daddy could only see me now!" Bill pulled Jenny to the floor and they danced for hours, only stopping to get another drink.

*

Jenny and Bill's second date was quite different and more secluded. They went for a hike and a picnic in Tilden Park in the Berkeley Hills. The couple walked along a quiet trail surrounded by indigenous redwoods and imported eucalyptus trees from Australia.

Light filtered through the forest as the warming sun played tag with the shadows. The two found a private little meadow off the trail behind blackberry and scrub oak bushes, staying carefully away from the poison oak.

Spreading a blanket on the grass, a bottle of Chateau Cheap wine was opened. They toasted with paper cups. Jenny said, "To the U.S. Navy." Bill laughed, "To those poor suckers still in Nam, come home alive." The wine went well with ham and cheese sandwiches. Bill produced a joint from his shirt pocket. He lit it took a toke and passed it to Jenny. She inhaled deeply.

The late summer air was cooled by the bay breezes and they snuggled for warmth. Bill kissed her, softly, shyly, seeking her invitation, then passionately, hunger growing as she kissed him back. Jenny stopped and looked at Bill like she was exploring his soul through his eyes. She smiled and kissed him playfully, biting his lip. He unbuttoned her blouse like a young boy opening a special gift for Christmas. He tried to remove her bra but couldn't unfasten the clasp in the back. She laughed. "Let me help you with that." She reached back and unclasped the lacy under garment. Her breasts were not large, not small and she self-consciously covered them with her arms folded in front.

Bill said, "You are so amazingly beautiful!"

A smile lit up her face and a cool wind caused goose bumps on her naked skin. He explored her body with his hands, then with his mouth. She rubbed her hands through his hair. "I'm on the pill," Jenny whispered in his ear as the rest of their clothing fell to the side of the blanket. She guided him to a place he never wanted to leave.

The sun climbed higher and warmed the naked couple. Bill explored with his fingers moving lightly along Jenny's body in the sexual afterglow. Jenny laid a hand on his chest and said softly, "Tell me about Nam."

"Are you sure? It's hard to talk about."

She nodded, cuddling.

"What do I tell you, about dead friends, body parts, blood and more blood? I was kind of on the outside, being the squad medic but I made some good friends…Let me tell you a story that changed everything about the war for me. We use to hang out in a bar in a small village near the river by the DMZ. I made friends with the bar girl named Twi. She was sweet, pretty and would take me back to her place. We listened to Beatles records and I would teach her English with the words of the songs."

"Did you have sex with her?" Jenny asked.

"Well yeah! Of course, you don't think we played Monopoly all night do you?"

"I was kinda hoping, Chutes and Ladders," she said with a giggle, and her hand grabbed him playfully.

He kissed her. "You delicious, southern bell I can't get enough of you."

"We're Navy people. How 'bout a game of Battleship?" She laughed, but stopped when she saw the pain in his eyes. "Sorry Bill, go on."

He gathered his thoughts and took a deep breath. "Anyway, on patrol one night we came under attack by the Viet Cong and gun fire was everywhere.

Mortar shells landed near us and a squad member was hit. I ran to him and bandaged his leg, applying pressure. I looked up at the dark VC soldiers and then I saw her, our eyes locked. It was Twi. She stopped for a millisecond and then rolled a grenade toward us. We dove out of the way just as it exploded."

"Oh my god!" Jenny whispered eyes wide open.

"Of course, I never saw her again. I started to wonder. What were we doing there? Who were the good guys and who were the bad guys? I was so confused."

They lay quietly for a few minutes. "Listen, I never really wanted to kill anyone, that's why I was a corpsman, but after that I could only count the days until my tour was up. War totally sucks! There is nothing good about it."

She could see the mist in his eyes as he looked far away.

He said, "I'm going to march in the anti-war protest in Berkeley on Labor Day. You are welcome to join me."

"Bill, you know I can't, you're discharged but I'm on active duty. If I got caught, I get in deep shit."

"I know lover, just thought I'd let you know." They held each other tight and she kissed him and playfully rolled on top of him.

*

The Labor Day Anti-War March started at Shattuck and University Avenue and was to proceed to the west end of the UC campus to the ROTC office where speeches were planned. Ten thousand people were expected but the crowd kept growing well past that number. Don, Wilkes and Bill arrived early and were in front. Bill was wearing his uniform, dress blues adorned with his medals, including a silver star. Organizers wanted him right in front with the other veterans so the TV cameras could see vets marching against the war, not just long haired hippie stereotypes. Don and Wilkes followed their buddy to the front of the crowd. By eight AM when the march started an estimated 75,000 people had gathered from all over the Bay Area. The Berkeley Police and Alameda County Sheriffs badly underestimated the numbers. They were caught unprepared for such a large crowd and looked worried.

The march started, a mass of humanity moving towards the university. It was more like a celebration than a march. People stood at the sides cheering and playing music with instruments or from boom boxes. Bob Dylan, John Lennon, Crosby, Stills and Nash protest songs accompanied the marchers. A group at the campus gate was pounding out a rhythm on conga drums.

As the marchers neared the ROTC building they could see it was surrounded by lines of police wearing riot helmets, billy clubs and tear gas at the ready.

A police captain with a loudspeaker announced to the protesters: "Disperse. This crowd is a safety hazard." Only the people in the front could hear him as more people poured in from the rear. People started chanting. "Hell no, we won't go! Hell no, we won't go!" The protesters pumped thousands of fists into the air.

"This is your last warning, DISPERSE."

"Maybe we should think about getting out of here," Bill said to Don and Wilkes.

Wilkes responded by chanting, "Hell no, we won't go," raising his fist, a big smile on his face.

Others started to provoke the police. "Fuck you pigs," yelled a bearded young man standing right next to Don. A rock landed among the officers.

The crowd kept growing bigger and people in the front were being pushed forward by the sea of humanity moving into the plaza. The police captain took action. He ordered his troopers forward and they came swinging batons. A sheriff came right at Bill, but seeing him in uniform walked past and took a swipe at Don, who ducked as the baton glanced off his shoulder.

The crowd surged at the police. They were seriously outnumbered and vulnerable. All of a sudden Bill heard the "thump" sound of a mortar round being fired. He instinctively yelled, "Incoming!" and dove to the ground. He quickly realized it was tear gas that was being fired and was almost trampled as the crowd started to scatter.

Wilkes helped Bill to his feet and the three started running toward Telegraph to the south.

An ocean of people swept like a tidal wave right behind them, eyes burning and choking from the gas.

"Don't stop, keep running!" Don yelled, as the three friends joined masses of people in full retreat as they left the campus and dashed down the street. Cars coming at them stopped horns blaring as the crowd surged into the avenue going the wrong way down a one way street. A fog of gas followed the escaping crowd enveloping Telegraph Avenue adding by-standers to the chaos. Don, Wilkes and Bill sprinted past the shopping district, then past the Co-op market. The boys kept moving trying to stay in front of the gas cloud.

They made it to their apartment and looked back to see people still scattering behind them in all directions. They went in, closed the windows, put wet towels against the cracks in the door and then took turns trying to wash the sting out of their eyes.

As Don sat down in the living room he turned to his buddies and said, "What the fuck just happened?"

*

Later that evening Don sat transfixed watching coverage of the march and the aftermath of on the local news. Bill was on the phone in the kitchen with Jenny telling her about the day. He had almost forgotten the interview he gave to the reporter before the march. Don yelled, "Bill, you're on the news."

Bill pulled the cord as far as it could reach and peeked at the cheap secondhand TV they had just purchased the day before so they could watch football and the World Series.

"Jenny tune your TV to the local news on channel 5," Bill told her over the phone.

That morning a reporter, Don James, had seen Bill in uniform, and asked if he would answer some questions.

"Sure," Bill said shrugging his shoulders but seeing the camera behind the reporter; he realized he might be on the news. He was here to protest the war, he thought, I might as well get on with it. That was before all hell broke loose.

Bill watched the interview unfold on the news.

Don James did an introduction then asked. "I see that you are in uniform. Are you in the Navy?"

"Just discharged."

"Did you go to Vietnam?"

"Yes sir. Spent a year as a corpsman in a combined Marine and Navy River Patrol Squadron."

"So why are you here at the protest?"

"I guess I got tired of watching my friends get killed or wounded."

"So you are against the war?"

"Yes sir. Listen, my Dad was in the Navy during World War II. I was proud to wear the uniform. I guess I'm still proud, I'm wearing it now. But this war is not World War II. I missed the part about the Vietnamese attacking Pearl Harbor."

"What about the notion that if South Vietnam falls it will have a domino effect and other countries will become communist?"

"It seems like our so-called allies aren't so happy with our war policies. If we get out of Vietnam more people in other countries will be friendly with the United States. The commies in the North of Vietnam will be quickly forgotten. Our government should be more worried about what the people of the United States think. Have you noticed there are a lot of people here protesting this war?"

"So there you have it from Bill Silver, someone just back from a tour in Vietnam. Back to you in the studio, Tom."

"Good job, Don, we will be back with more news after these commercial announcements."

"So now I'm dating a TV star," Jenny said.

"Maybe you shouldn't tell people on the base that you're dating that guy."

"Who? Never met that guy."

"Don't worry; they won't recognize me in civvies when I pick you up Friday night."

"Oh, you think I am going to go out with you again after that newscast?"

"Yup."

"And why is that?"

"You have to admit I looked good in uniform

on the TV."

Jenny laughed out loud. "Okay handsome, I guess you all can come around this weekend. Bye Bill."

"Bye Jenny."

*

September is usually the warmest month in the Bay Area. But the day of the fall equinox the sky filled with fog, chilling any underdressed, unaware tourist to the bone. Laura Goldman blew into town like a winter storm. To Don and his friends, his big sister was a ray of sunshine.

No one knew she was coming. Laura had taken a Greyhound bus across the country and arrived in Oakland wearing just shorts and a t-shirt. By the time local transit deposited her to the Telegraph Avenue apartment she was freezing. She leaned on the door buzzer. Wilkes answered, "Who's there?"

"John Booth, you get me out of this cold windy fog."

"Who is it?"

"Laura."

"Laura who?"

"Laura Goldman, you ditz."

"Holy shit!" He hit the buzzer and let the object of his high school fantasies into the apartment.

Laura came into the flat grabbed a throw blanket and folded her long slender 23 year-old body into a living room chair. Her long brown hair fell down to her shoulders and her brown eyes sparkled as she asked, "Where is my little brother?"

"Out working, he got a temporary job selling Fuller Brush products door to door in San Leandro. Did he tell you we are planning to stay here awhile?"

"Yea, I was wondering if I could crash with you guys a little while. I made some plans to go to graduate school just north of here."

"I'm sure you could crash here for a while. What college? Where?"

"Have you heard of Sonoma State College? It's about fifty miles north. They have a great humanistic psychology program. You know Don dropped out of Yale last spring, hated economics, I thought he might want to join me, try psych or something. What about you?"

"I never went to college, had a pretty good job as an apprentice plumber, good money, union, but I couldn't see working in Queens the rest of my life. I've got some money in the bank so I just came along for the ride. Don't know if college is my thing, but I'm ready to check out some new stuff, if you know what I mean."

"Yeah, sure, me too, that's why I'm here." She shivered a little. The cold made her nipples hard noticeable against the cotton fabric of her shirt. Laura giggled, noticing that Wilkes was glancing lower than her eyes during their conversation. "John Wilkes Booth, are you checking out my boobs?"

His face flushed red, "To tell you the truth Laura they are not hard to notice."

"I'm wet and cold and I need a hot shower." Laura pulled her clingy t-shirt over her head, her breasts peeking out at the younger man. She chuckled and headed to the bathroom as her hips swayed walking away from him. She said, "I remember when you used to look at me when I was a senior and you were a sophomore. Keep those thoughts Wilkes, you just might get lucky yet."

The bathroom door closed, the water started and all Wilkes could do was sit there and say, "Wow!"

A minute later he heard her yell from the shower, "Hey, John Wilkes, there's a spot on my back I can't reach."

*

Bill spent the day hiking in Tilden Park. He liked walking in the cool foggy almost drizzly weather, so unlike the warm monsoons in Vietnam. The wet bay leaves gave off a spicy smell. He stopped and looked at the place he and Jenny had made love for the first time. As he stood there, he thought he heard someone crying. He went to the sound. In the tangled berry bushes and found a little black and white puppy whimpering and shivering.

Bill looked around but saw no other animals

or people. "Where is your mama little pup?" He reached out and picked up the little puppy, seeing it was a male, probably just a few months old. Bill hugged the wet ball of fur to his chest, looked around again and yelled, "Hello anyone out there missing a dog?" No answer arrived, just the sound of the leaves dripping.

The puppy licked his face and he asked, "What am I going to do with you? I can't leave you to be a snack for a coyote. Now can I?"

He carried the pup back to the parking lot, placed him on the seat next to him in his newly acquired used car. Bill had purchased a 1968 AMC station wagon two days earlier. Not his first choice but all he could afford from his back military pay. He slapped a peace sticker on the back window to give the car some personality. The dog snuggled against his thigh as he drove down the hill to the freeway to pick up Jenny at Treasure Island.

Bill drove to the barracks and Jenny ran to the car, opened the door, slid into the passenger seat and noticed the little orphan between them. "Where did you find that?"

"In the park, real close to the place where you seduced me. Do you like dogs?"

Jenny laughed, "I seduced you huh? Okay, stud, I'll let that go. We had a pointer growing up, my dad use to go bird hunting with her. I loved that dog."

"Well, I think I'm taking him home. I never had a dog."

"Ya'll gotta name picked out?"

"I don't know if I'll ever get use to you saying 'ya'al', but it sure sounds cute coming from you."

"Just cause you're a damn Yankee boy, you don't have to give me crap about the way I talk." She punched him in the arm flirtatiously.

"You know it just turns me on?"

"Well in that case, what are **ya'll** going to name that little mutt?" Jenny laughed overplaying her accent.

"What do you think about Tilden? That way whenever I say his name I'll think of you and the first day we made love."

"You know, for a damn Yankee ya'll can be pretty romantic." She kissed him on the cheek.

*

Don and Millie dated a few more times, had some fun, nothing serious. When Millie broke it off, Don was more relieved than disappointed.

The night Bill brought Tilden home, Bill, Don and Jenny sat in the living room passing around a joint, a New York thin crust pizza was sitting in a box on the table waiting for them to get the munchies. They could hear the hushed talking and giggling coming from Wilkes' room as the puppy tried to eat the leg off the second-hand table.

Laura tiptoed behind Don and covered his eyes with her hands. "Guess who?" she said, trying to disguise her voice. She was dressed in Wilkes' large Grateful Dead t-shirt that barely covered her privates but showed all of her shapely legs.

"Laura! Is that you?" Don asked, jumping to his feet.

"Surprise!" she said and threw a bear hug on her startled sibling.

"What…how…why?" Don stammered planting a fat kiss on her cheek.

Wilkes joined them as Laura explained her acceptance to grad school, the bus trip, and her earlier arrival.

Bill asked, "How did you two wind up in the bedroom?"

Wilkes shrugged, blushing, his face frozen in a wide grin.

Laura said, "I was cold, wet, and needed a hot shower and the way John Wilkes has been looking at me since he reached puberty, I thought it might be fun to offer him a bite off the apple."

They all took a minute to digest Laura's free love explanation.

"So Sonoma State, where in the world is that?" Bill asked Laura as they started to eat the pizza, "Do you even know how to get there?"

"Navy boy, you can read a map for me, can't you?"

Wilkes said, "Hey Don and I just navigated across the country didn't we? We'll get you there."

"Sounds like a road trip. I can take you on Monday," Don said.

Bill turned to Jenny, "Can you get Monday off?"

"I'm sure I can trade duty with someone."

They spread a big California map out in front of them.

*

Later when they were in bed, Bill went to kiss Jenny but she turned her head, pretending to be a little jealous. "I saw the way you looked at Laura."

"Darlin' you are wonderful, beautiful and I'm totally into you, but the only way I don't look at a woman as lovely as Laura with all that leg showing is when I'm dead."

She laughed at his honesty, kissed him hungrily. They moved together, exploring in foreplay, passions igniting; but were interrupted by Tilden whimpering, looking longingly at the couple and wanting up on the bed. Bill laughed threw a pillow on the floor for the little mutt. "I don't need any help from you tonight, Tilden, you can sleep on that." The pup circled the cushiony mound twice before settling comfortably on his new soft bed. "I think I've got a smart dog there. Where were we?"

Jenny giggled, "You were kissing me here," she pointed.

*

Road trip time. The five plus the puppy piled into Bill's station wagon and headed across the Richmond San Rafael Bridge, through Marin County, up highway 101, to the unknown frontier of Sonoma County.

"Why did you think of applying to Sonoma State College?" Jenny asked Laura.

"I heard about their psychology program. It's cutting edge, very Gestalt."

"I have no idea what that is. What's Gestalt?" she asked Laura.

"A simple way of explaining it is that you get in touch with your feelings, using different techniques. You go deep into your psyche to find out what hurts. Hopefully then with help you work to cure that problem."

"I guess that makes sense," Jenny said.

"The other reason I chose this college, I heard that Sonoma State is in the redwoods, rural countryside, yet close enough hop on a bus back to San Francisco. I want to live in a place closer to nature, spread out and relax but I'm a city girl at heart. I may need to return to the urban jungle to play. Do you know what nick name the students gave the school? Granola U. Doesn't that sound perfect?" Laura said with a laugh.

Jenny nodded. "I think I know what you mean."

Wilkes gazed at Laura in the back seat with a sense of longing. Two evenings earlier, Saturday night, Wilkes suggested that the two of them should ball again. Laura smiled gave him a peck on the cheek and said, "Wilkes, I had fun with you but I really don't want any attachments, okay? I had a boyfriend back east, but right now I need to be free."

Wilkes had looked at her face, her body, down to her toes, and said with regret, "Sure. If that's what you want."

She smiled at her younger brother's friend and said, "That leaves you free. You're really quite a catch."

Wilkes replied, "Yeah, well freedom's just another word for nothing left to lose."

Laura laughed. "I guess that makes me Janis and you must be Bobby McGee."

Wilkes sighed, and returned to the present moment, the Janis tune playing in his head, as Bill turned off the freeway at the Cotati exit. They drove through the small downtown to Rohnert Park, a brand new suburban area that had grown around the young college.

The five unloaded from the station wagon, put Tilden on a leash and walked onto a campus that represented a new generation. Laura and Don immediately saw the difference from the ivy covered brick buildings of the universities they had attended back East. The trees planted between the cement buildings were young, not full grown. There was space to spread out. The vibe given off by the students lacked the competitive Ivy League tension.

At eleven o'clock in the morning on the Monday when they had arrived, Frisbees filled the air. It seemed like a major student occupation. Both young males and females, barefoot, were tossing discs in the open areas between buildings, showing off an athleticism previously only seen on the fields of NCAA intercollegiate sports. One-hundred-foot tosses were followed by running catches behind the back.

Don, Laura, and Bill went to meet with college counselors, while Jenny and Wilkes explored the campus, Tilden in tow. The two new friends walked to the far side of the university and found a small duck pond surrounded by young redwood trees.

"What are you going to do if they move up here to go to school?" Jenny asked.

"I haven't decided yet. I don't think I'll go back to New York. I read an article in the *San Francisco Chronicle* about the ski resorts needing workers for the winter. We drove through this mountain town, Truckee. It was just down from a place called Squaw Valley. As nice as it is here, there's something about the Sierra Mountains that seems special to me. What about you? Will you and Bill stay together?"

"I have two years left in the Navy. I haven't told Bill yet, but I've received orders for my next duty station, at the Newport, Rhode Island submarine base.

"You're kidding, what will you do?"

"What can I do?"

"Do you like being in the Navy?"

"It's not bad. I like the travel and meeting new people. I wanted to get away from home. After my mom died, my dad started drinking a lot. He could be a mean drunk but so sweet at the other times. He was a Navy lifer and I was daddy's little girl. I love him so much, but I can't be around him anymore. I guess when he retired from the Navy and mom died, he didn't know what to do, so he drank."

"Did he hit you?"

"Twice. After the first time, he cried and apologized to me the next morning. The second time, I just went out and joined the Navy the next day.

"What did your mom die from?"

"Lung cancer."

"Did she smoke?"

"Yeah," The two were quiet for a few minutes watching the ducks.

"When are you going to tell Bill?"

"Tonight when we get back."

"Without you in the Bay Area, he'll probably want to move up here with Don and Laura."

*

The young couple held each other at the gate of San Francisco International Airport. Tears filled Jenny's eyes. "Tell me one more time that you love me."

Bill whispered in her ear, "I always will love you."

"I don't want you mooning over me. I'll write but we are going to be away from each other for a long time."

"We could get married you know."

"Don't think I didn't check it out. My horoscope says it's not a good time. If we are both free in two years when I get out…well, we'll see."

UNITED AIRLINES FLIGHT 110
FROM SAN FRANCISCO TO BOSTON
NOW BOARDING GATE 19.

Jenny waited till all the other passengers went down the ramp, then looked up and kissed Bill gently on the lips. "Ya'll take care now."

She turned from him, gave the attendant the ticket and walked away. Bill felt his head grow dizzy, and he sat down for a second. He watched the plane pull away from the gate and tug on his heartstrings. It took off, getting smaller as Jenny flew out of his life.

Chapter 4

The Penngrove Ponderosa

On October 12, 1972, Rick Cartwright turned twenty-eight years old. The successful real estate agent had little reason to celebrate. He had all the toys. A Mercedes sedan for him while his wife drove around in a Porsche. An extravagant pool sat in the elegantly landscaped backyard behind the Cartwright's large, lavish house in Tiburon. All the wealth and possessions left Rick unhappy and unfulfilled.

Rick's perfectly fashioned wife Cheryl avoided having children by faithfully taking the pill. She told anyone that would listen at the trendy parties that she was not ready to give up her girlish figure and settle down to a life of station wagons full of snot nosed kids.

After Rick told her that he no longer wanted to be on the express to the Marin County's gravy train, she told him she wanted a divorce. They divided the assets. Cheryl's lawyer made sure she kept the Marin estate. In turn Rick was able to make a land investment of his own. He bought a small old ranch house on few acres of land four miles southeast of the Sonoma State campus, near the little town of Penngrove.

Growing up in California, Rick always found the earth's rumblings interesting so he enrolled at Sonoma State as a geology major in the fall of 1973. The divorcee was looking for roommates when the extraordinary woman named Laura showed up at his door and would change his life.

"I called you about your ad at the college for roommates."

"Come in. Do you want something to drink?" he asked.

"No thanks." She sat in a chair across from him. "Are you a student?" Laura asked.

"Yes, and I own this house, but I want to rent out the empty rooms. You said on the phone that you might have some friends that are interested."

"Yes, my brother and his good friend. By the way, would you allow a dog?"

"Sure, actually this place could use a dog. So you might want to rent out all three empty rooms?"

"Yes," she said tentatively, "but I need to know some stuff about you."

"Okay, what would you like to know?"

She smiled. "I'm getting a good vibe from you. You're not an ax murderer are you?"

Rick laughed, "Only on slow weekends."

"Would you mind if I did some decorating?"

He looked up at his naked walls and a lack of

window coverings in the living room and laughed. "This place definitely looks like it needs a woman's touch doesn't it?"

Laura pulled a joint out of her pocket and asked, "You got a match?"

He knew this unusual and lovely women dressed in pink tennis shoes, snug bell bottoms and a Rolling Stones tee shirt complete with Mick Jagger's lips was testing his limits. He lit the joint and they passed it. "So tell me about your brother and his friend."

"Don, my brother, dropped out of Yale University as an economics major last year. He is starting at Sonoma as a psych major. Bill is a Vietnam vet, Navy medic, and has been given two years college credit towards a nursing degree."

He took another hit off the joint and passed it back to her. "What about you?"

"I'm a psych grad student working on a Masters in social work. What are you studying?"

"Geology, I started in July, summer school. Bought this place in June and I have been fixing it up."

"Why geology?"

"To tell you the truth, I love learning about nature and the earth. Here in California we have so much tectonic activity. I took classes about it at Marin JC years ago, so I'm starting here as a junior"

"So, Mr. Cartwright, where's Little Joe?"

"Gee, I never heard that one before," he replied smiling. "When do I meet Don and Bill?"

"They're at the campus, we are meeting later. I'll bring them by if that's okay."

"Sounds good."

By the way," she asked, "where did you hide Hoss?"

"You really think that this place is like the TV show *Bonanza*'s Ponderosa?"

"The Penngrove Ponderosa, I like that."

Rick immediately liked Laura. She was a woman as different from his ex-wife as night and day. Her personality drew people in like North attracts a compass.

They all moved in the next week. It was just a

day before the new school year of 1974.

*

Redwood trees towered above them, the autumn day a crispy cool and the water steaming. The four new roommates lay in the hot springs in the hills above Dry Creek Valley. "Have you ever been naked with two other guys?" Laura asked Rick.

"Not since my high school football locker room."

Bill asked, "What position did you play?"

"Linebacker, defense—wingback, offense.

"What's a wingback?" Don asked Rick.

"It's like a flanker but you line up behind the tight-end."

"Boring!" Laura exclaimed.

"What?" Don asked.

"Please, are we really going to soak in this beautiful spot and talk about football?" As she lay back her breasts seemed to float on the water and she was tickled when she noticed Rick and Bill staring at her nipples. "Do you want to know what position I played the last time I was naked with two guys? Tight end and wide receiver."

"Oh man sis, really you want to talk about that in front of me?"

Bill and Rick were laughing, partly at the joke and partly at Don's discomfort.

"Well Don it was a joke, chill out. But seriously we are going to be living together and we're not kids anymore. I have to know that I'm free to be me, or we can't live together."

"Okay, you have a point but Sis I love you and want to protect you. It's hard to let that go, to think that my big sister was having sex with all types of guys…yuck!"

"Haven't you heard of sexual liberation?"

"Of course, maybe I'll have sex with two women. How would you feel about that?"

Laura laughed. "Proud of my little brother. You go for it."

Bill said, "Pass me some more of that wine. This has to be the best stuff I ever tasted."

They had stopped at Creek Winery, which had

only been open for a few years. The winery was one of the first in the incredibly beautiful Dry Creek Valley. Most of the valley land was covered in apple orchards. The green hillsides were covered by towering redwood trees. In the hills were natural hot springs bubbling into pools and looking out at the redwood forest. The winery was closed for Veteran's Day, but the winemaker had been out front and asked them to help move some boxes in exchange for a few bottles of wine. The college students were more than happy to do some work for a couple of bottles of Chardonnay and Cabernet.

Rick asked Laura "Have you really been with two guys?"

The young naked woman thought for a second. Did she want to share this story with these guys? Finally she said, "Last year I was with my boyfriend, Joey, in the Village. We were at a friend's party. The party got a little crazy and lots of fun. Some people were taking MDA and Joey and I took some. Clothing became optional and at midnight Joey and I found we were in a big bathtub full of champagne with two other couples. We were all kissing and feeling each other. Joey and I watched as others made love and then we had sex in the tub, drinking champagne and pouring it on each other." Laura paused as tears welled up in her eyes. "Two days later, Joey jumped off a twenty-story building." She cried chest heaving. She lay naked and vulnerable in front of them. They were quiet, letting her cry for a few minutes. The smell of the sulfur spring was strong, like it was powerful enough to cleanse her emotional wound.

Rick finally said, "Laura that's so sad. If you ever need a friend to talk to I'm right here."

"I found a note in his bedroom, 'I'll never ever be able to get that high again.' I loved him. But I'm so angry. I don't know if I'm making any sense." Then she said with a brave smile, "Come on pour me some more wine and pass me a joint. I'm tired of being a buzzkill."

Chapter 5
The Acid Experiment

The first autumn rain fell outside the Penngrove Ponderosa, cleansing the dust that topped everything during the long summer drought. Water flooded streets as autumn leaves clogged drains long unused. The brown golden grasses would soon turn Irish green as the desperate flora rootstock drank like students on free beer night in the local pub.

All things out of the comfort of the house seeped and soaked in the flow of rainwater but the old ranchhouse stayed dry and warm. An oak fire blazed casting long shadows on the now tastily covered walls. Laura kept it simple and inexpensive using framed posters a mix of framed rock music interspersed with an eclectic mix, modern and classical posters of works of art.

Rick called a family meeting and asked everyone to come into the living room. "I don't want to be the king of the house. Let's make some ground rules."

Laura said, "I'm certainly not going to play the woman's traditional role of cooking and cleaning."

Bill said, "Okay, let's make a chore list."

"How bout we take turns cooking and cleaning up?" suggested Don.

Laura said, "That won't work. There are seven week days and only four of us."

Don had an idea. "What if we share the cost and buy groceries together Monday through Thursday. We all take a night cooking and cleaning, but on weekends everybody's on their own."

"Great thinking. I'll be happy to make a chore list," Rick volunteered. "If you agree raise your hand."

All hands went up.

"What about having friends over? Does anybody have any problems with that?" Bill asked.

Rick said, "I don't see any problems as long as everyone is responsible for their own guests."

There was some more give and take of ideas until a plan was democratically adopted.

Laura said, "Can I change the subject? I'm planning on doing a little psych experiment on myself, try a little self-exploration. I have three tabs of acid and I'm going to get high for three days straight. Would you guys be willing to respect my space, not talk to me? Let me be me. Just check to see I don't go over the deep end."

The three men looked at her with open mouths.

"Really?" Don asked his big sister.

Laura said, "Believe it or not this is a school project. I know, not exactly the scientific method, but

I don't have the time or money for a control group. Sometimes you have got to be your own guinea pig; besides, if Timothy Leary did it at Harvard, I would think I could experiment at Sonoma State.

Rick said, "It's okay with me, if that's what you want. I'm just a little worried about you."

"That's sweet Rick. Now stop worrying."

*

Laura fasted that night, cleansing her body and started her acid test the next morning. Naked, she lit a fire and gazed at it for hours. The flames were alive, jumping, popping, licking and consuming the wood like it was a feast at a party for two. It tempted Laura, saying, "Come play with me."

Laura laughed in the face of the fire. "You stay right where you are you son of the Devil. I've seen evil men like you before."

The rain continued. Wrapped in a blanket, she tip-toed silently to the window to watch that show. Each drop on the glass pane shimmered and danced, some joining with another in wet embrace.

She slipped back to the fire and placed a

crystal ball on a stand in front of the dancing flames. Pictures of past, present and future played on the ball like a special television show illuminating her mind. Laura noticed the boys peeking over to see her stare at the glass orb, so she slipped over to give each a kiss on the cheek.

Looking at her image in a mirror she saw her brown eyes speckled with gold, her long brown hair curled and frizzed. Her smile radiated the warmth of the fire. About noon she felt like dancing. She put Beethoven on the stereo, threw down the blanket and pranced wildly for what seemed like hours, feeling her body glistening in glorious sweat, her mouth so thirsty.

Taking a drink, she felt the water play its way down soothing her throat, then felt it circle the esophagus to her stomach where it stayed and tickled.

Rewrapped in the blanket she returned to the crystal ball show in front of the fire.

Time had no meaning and her body had no hunger, so no food crossed her lips. Exhaustion captured her, bed beckoning like a lost lover. She went falling into the pillowed cloud and crashed hard.

The next morning's sky awoke clear and cool. Laura, up with the dawn, took her magic pill, and watched the light bite at the darkness. The royal sun god rose over the hills in the early sky. Adorned in a big wool sweater, showing colors that would have made the Bible's Joseph jealous, she set out walking up the road to the top of Sonoma Mountain. Laura watched yesterday's raindrops tumble from a tall redwood tree's needles. The clearing wind blew oak and sycamore leaves past her feet. The newly naked branches of those trees waved saying, good morning. She noticed things that one never sees in day-to-day life. Laura walked all day not eating but drinking grape juice from a big canteen slung over her shoulder. With each step, she felt like she was making a new discovery. In the evening her body spent from the climb and descent, she quietly slipped back into the house, back to her room, and fell into a dreamless sleep.

On day three, the ants came out of their hill in a long straight line to find a food source twenty yards away and shouldered a bundle bigger than their bodies. The workers would then circle to carry the burden and return in parallel straight lines back to the hill. Laura thought, Wow! That's just what we can see aboveground. Focusing, she saw the underground caves leading to the queen. Glorious! she heard herself say. Laura studied this anthill, not knowing how much time had passed but seeing the sun moved well past midmorning.

Her dark brown hair felt frizzier each day she took the drug and while the sky clouded, her mind became clear. She came to California to move away from her grief and feelings of guilt from the suicide of her boyfriend. She had loved being a New York girl. Now she was letting the beauty of Northern California sink into her soul. She was no longer getting away from something. Freedom rang its liberty bell. She was here and now and she loved it.

Laura looked across the road as the black and white stallion trotted over to a tan mare. He nuzzled her, his enormous penis extended. He bit the mare on the neck and Laura imagined the mare's musty smell invading the male's nostrils. The stallion mounted the mare and the female horse looked at Laura and said "It doesn't get any better than this, girl."

Laughing, she turned away from the equine lovers and went back to her new home.

Rick was eating a sandwich in the kitchen.

Laura ended her meditative chemical monk-like silence and asked, "Rick, do you know what you want to do with the field behind the house?"

"You are back from your trip?"

"Yes, I'm still a little up but I took a Valium."

"You okay?"

"More than okay, I'm feeling super. This brings me back to my question about the field."

"I have no plans. Why?"

"I want to get a horse. It's been a long time since I've felt the reins in my hands."

"Okay, but you're responsible," Rick Cartwright said, "You think this is really the Ponderosa."

"I don't think it's the TV's Ponderosa. It's our very own Penngrove Ponderosa."

Chapter 6

Brownies

Laura received a stipend of three hundred dollars a month as a grad student and teacher's aide. Bill, living on the GI bill received a check from the VA for two hundred dollars a month. Room rent at the Penngrove Ponderosa was seventy five dollars a month, for each roommate. So Laura and Bill learned to live frugally, eating lots of beans and peanut butter and jelly sandwiches.

In the Sonoma State world of the early seventies, most students lived cheaply. T-shirts and cutoffs were the usual summertime attire, while sweatshirts and jeans worked in the winter. Many students looked for bargains at the Salvation Army, used clothing stores or military surplus. Unable to afford gas and insurance, Bill sold his car and bought a bicycle.

Don was in bigger financial trouble. His parents had saved money to send him to college but when he dropped out of Yale they cut him off, barely on speaking terms. When Don told his parents he was going back to school in California, he asked about support. His father told Don and Laura that he refused to support their hippie lifestyles. "Cut your hair and get a job."

Don needed money and he found his solution as an entrepreneur. Unfortunately, his business was not legal. He sold brownies—marijuana brownies. He baked each night and sold individual brownies the next day. Repeat business was very good as word spread underground, around the campus.

Don delivered an order to a room where geology students hung out between classes on the third floor of the Darwin Building. Rick was in the room studying with four other classmates, two guys and two girls. He introduced the group to his roommate and suggested that they take a break. Don zoomed in on Kathy, immediately infatuated. She returned his gaze.

She was tiny, maybe ninety pounds. He guessed she was part Asian or Native American, yet had striking blue eyes. While Don was wearing Levis and a green military jacket, the typical hippie uniform, Kathy dressed in a bright golden skirt, knee-high boots, a starched white blouse with a light blue neckerchief to complete the mod look, like she could be a go-go dancer at a disco.

"Are you geology major?" Don asked trying to strike up a conversation.

She answered. "Yup, best department in the school, love the classes, great teachers." She smiled at him. He melted.

"So you're into earthquakes?"

"This science is a lot more then earthquakes. But yeah, earthquakes and moving plates are interesting."

"Well, I've learned a little bit about it just living with Rick."

"Oh, are you the brownie man?"

Don looked around slightly paranoid.

"Don't worry, I'm cool. Rick has shared some of your brownies with me and some other students. He told me about you. It's good to meet you in person. What are you studying?"

Don looked into her swimming pool blue eyes and said to Kathy, "Right now it's psychology. I just transferred from back east and changed my major from economics."

"Do you like it?"

"I'm not sure, still exploring I guess. I hope you don't mind me asking, you look Asian but you have blue eyes."

"I don't mind, people have always asked me about my eyes. My dad is white, mom's Korean. She was a war bride. Of course these days, people think I'm Vietnamese."

"I think you're uniquely beautiful, if you don't mind me saying so."

"That's sweet."

"How would you like to go get a cup of coffee?"

"Only if you provide the brownie," Kathy said with a tantalizing smile.

*

Kathy lived in the dorms. As love bloomed between the two vertically-challenged students, she spent many hours visiting at the Penngrove Ponderosa. The two got a good laugh when they discovered they both saved money buying children's sized clothing.

They were together baking on April 1, 1974, when Laura came home early from school and interrupted them.

"Don, one of the professors I worked with

warned me that the police have a raid planned for tomorrow. You're going to be busted."

"Yeah, sure, good one. I know it's April first, good joke."

"I'm not joking! You have to listen. I'm supposed to be teaching a class right now. I left it early to warn you. I'm not kidding. Do you know where Rick is? We've got to let him know."

"I still don't believe you. How would this guy know and why would he tell you?"

"Because, you bozo, the professor's brother is on the Cotati Police and he actually uses your brownies so he doesn't want to bust you, but the Feds are involved."

Laura tried to leave a message for Rick to call her with somebody in the geology department, but she hung up the phone when she noticed Rick pulling up with Bill in the car. Don and Kathy quit cooking. The group sat down in the living room.

After hearing from Laura, Rick asked, "How much marijuana do you have left?"

"About a pound and I still have to pay my

dealers for it."

Bill asked, "Could we put it in a plastic baggy, take it out in the field and bury it?"

Rick said, "Not if they use drug dogs. They'll find it."

Laura suggested, "Maybe we should burn it all right now in the fireplace."

Don protested, "That's a lot of good stuff going up in smoke, and I would be out a lot of money."

It was Kathy that offered a solution. "Why don't we cook it up in a big spaghetti sauce, put it in jars. I know enough people in the dorms that could hold it for you. Or maybe they would just want to buy a jar."

So Laura and Bill went off to the Rohnert Park Safeway for tomatoes, spices, onions, garlic, canning jars, and large cooking pots. That night as the five of them simmered sauce, they consumed much of the cooking wine. Laura provided a great New York Italian recipe from a friend in Brooklyn. They were afraid the house phone was tapped, so Kathy went to the pay phone in Penngrove to call people to help stash the sauce.

By morning, all the marijuana was cooked into the sauce and the Ponderosa smelled like the best Italian restaurant in North Beach. Still paranoid, they took turns driving the sauce to the dorms in a circular route, watching to make sure no one was following. Then they cleaned the house from top to bottom, getting rid of any traces of drugs.

April 2nd and 3rd came without any hint of a raid. Nothing happened. The students went back to their classes trying to act normal. Don wondered if Laura had been fed some false information.

At exactly 0600 (police time) on April 5th the task force knocked and broke into the front and back doors. The Penngrove Ponderosa was under assault. Five cars were parked out front—two marked Sonoma County Sheriff, one Cotati Police, two big green unmarked Fords unloading men with jackets marked ATF and FBI. The raiders were serious, guns drawn. Rick answered the door rubbing sleep from his eyes. "We have warrants to search this place. DON

GOLDMAN?" the sheriff called out.

"Yes," Don answered and stepped forward.

"We have an arrest warrant for you." The young officer handcuffed Don and read him his rights.

Rick asked the officer, "Where are you taking him?"

"The county court house in Santa Rosa."

Laura got on the phone and called the attorney they had put on retainer. The law enforcement people searched for hours. They had been told to look for brownies and, of course, they didn't find any. They also didn't find any other drugs. The agents left the place a mess. Flour was on the kitchen floor, coffee was poured out on the table. Books were scattered about. They brought in a drug dog while Tilden was taken into the back yard. The dog gave many false hits to his handler but still they found nothing. The police went out to the field with Chardonnay, Laura's horse and even examined the horse manure.

Finally, anti-climatically, the invasion force left the house, sat in their cars, filling out forms hoping that maybe a buyer or seller would show up at the house. At 1400 the six cars pulled out quietly telling no one. No white flag was raised but the Penngrove Ponderosa stood invaded but unconquered like Vietnam.

Rick found the flag he usually hung on the Fourth of July and hung it by the damaged front door. He then drove up to Santa Rosa and by 4 PM (Pacific civilian time) Don was out on bail.

Two weeks later the lawyer called to say the case had been dropped for lack of evidence. After selling off all the spaghetti sauce, Don would have plenty of money to make it through the semester. Unfortunately for those students looking for more spaghetti sauce with a special zest, he would be looking for a new line of work.

*

They were unlikely best friends, four foot eleven inch Kathy and a foot taller Laura. They were both beautiful, with personalities as different as their sizes. Laura was the outgoing, flirtatious postgraduate psychology major. Kathy was quiet, almost introverted and the girlfriend of the young man they both loved, in different ways.

It was a cool, crisp, late April evening, the stars were out and Laura's Don was home working on a paper about the influence of Buddha on Carl Jung. It was times like this that he remembered why he dropped out of Yale.

The girls were in the Keg Room, a pub that was a favorite student bar in downtown Cotati. Beers were served in a cold mug and were only fifty cents. While Sonoma State was located in Rohnert Park, little Cotati only a few miles away was the place where students went to hang out. Unbelievably, the intersection of downtown streets formed a peace sign, coming together in a circle around a Y. The city had been built long before the anti-war movement of the late sixties and early seventies.

The two girls had been nursing beers and munching pretzels for two hours discussing religion, sex, and politics. Two bold young men came up and the blond one said, "Can I buy you girls a beer?"

Laura looked the young man up and down and said, "Aren't you the big spender? You mean you've got a whole buck to spend on two beautiful women. Trying to get lucky, are you?"

"Hey, we're just college students looking to have a good time."

Laura looked at both the well-muscled blond and the dark chiseled quiet one standing on the opposite side of the table and said, "Yeah, you guys aren't bad, but she's got a boyfriend and I'm a little tired, so one of you has to go home."

The young man laughed but made no retreat. Laura looked at Kathy and shrugged her shoulders.

"Okay, sit down and buy us a beer if you want, but my boyfriend's going to be here in an hour. Hey, I've seen you on campus," Kathy said to the brown-haired boy. "You were playing ultimate Frisbee in front of Darwin. You're a good player. I'm Kathy and that's Laura."

The dark one said, "I'm Derek and that's Luke." He sat down as Luke went to the bar to get a pitcher. He turned to Laura and said, "You know, if you're too tired, we could both come back tomorrow night."

"Touche! Okay wise guy, I'm going to say it. Do you come here often?"

"Yeah, we do. The beer is cold, cheap, and the owner Jim has offered to sponsor our softball team in city league."

"You looking for players?" Kathy asked Luke as he returned with the brew.

"Sorry, it's not a coed team but there are girl and coed leagues if you want to play."

"No, I'm not interested, but we have three guy roommates who were jocks in high school."

"Three guy roommates, you weren't kidding about being tired," Derek said.

"Hey now, one of those guys is my brother and her boyfriend. The other two…are just friends."

"Do you know what positions they play?" Luke asked.

"They'll be here soon. You can ask them." said Laura.

They talked about Frisbee, softball, and

classes at the school as an hour scooted by. Laura's three roommates came into the bar.

Kathy got up and kissed Don who said, "It's sure nice to have a girlfriend I don't have to get on my tip-toes to kiss." Kathy just smiled looking up into his eyes.

Laura said, "These two guys are starting up a softball team. I told them you guys might want to play."

Derek said, "We are starting practice next week at the park in Cotati. You guys come out."

Bill said, "Sounds like fun. I miss playing ball." They worked out the details and the seven continued to talk and drink beer.

*

The alarm went off and Laura woke up hung-over, cotton-mouthed, and groggy. She felt the body in bed with her before she opened her eyes. The fog around her brain struggled to clear. What was his name? Derek? Yeah, fuckin' Derek. Shit, I don't need this now. I need to be in class in less than an hour. She shook the man-boy in her bed.

"WAKE UP!" Laura demanded, sitting up, her naked breasts sitting level to the cute but blurry eyes of the now unwelcome guest in her bed. "You're Derek right? You know, I can barely remember leaving the Keg Room. I hope I made you buy me dinner."

"We didn't have dinner."

"Oh, that's why I feel so bad. Listen, sweetie, I'm sure you're a great guy, but I'm late for class. I've got to go, so let yourself out."

Laura got up and jogged naked to the shower, turned the water on very hot, then cold. She shivered and came out to see the boy was back asleep in her big brass bed. Laura just shrugged, pulled on her bell bottom jeans, not bothering with underwear, a tie-dyed cotton long sleeve pullover, no bra, purple and pink striped socks with sandals. Racing to the kitchen, she grabbed a cup of coffee and sauntered out the door jumping into the car with Rick. He held out two aspirin.

"Thanks, you're a lifesaver."

Chapter 7
Great White Sharks and Other Demons

Bill felt reborn as he took his picnic lunch into the quad area. Friday afternoon classes ended and a local band was blasting rock and roll in front of the science building. Students free for the weekend's festivities danced, played Frisbee or just hung out in the early spring sunshine. The smell of marijuana spiced the air as joints and cups of cheap wine were being passed around.

Bill loved college life. He studied hard and played hard. Not a great student in high school, he learned to thrive in the university atmosphere. Discipline that he did not have in his earlier education, he had learned in the Navy. Classes were tough but fascinating. He soaked up knowledge like spring sunshine. Even the English class that he had to take as a graduation requirement expanded his mind. Shakespeare could be interesting? Who knew?

The horror of Vietnam seemed like a bad dream from long ago. The nightmares still sometimes haunted his darkest thoughts, but the bright spring sunlight of this glorious Sonoma afternoon flowed through his body, cleansing his soul.

He sat toward the back of the quad, pulled out a tuna sandwich and took a bite. While his mouth enjoyed the taste of the food, his eyes and ears consumed the full flavor of the springtime festivities.

"You're blocking the sun."

Bill had not even noticed the young woman lying on a blanket behind him when he sat down. He was too busy taking in the big scene of the Friday concert. She was petite, blonde, beautiful, and only a pair of pink nylon short shorts kept her from being totally naked. How could I have not noticed this angelic figure when I sat down, he wondered.

"Sorry," he said as he moved beside her, giving him a better view of her naked firm breasts and lovely legs. Her eyes were closed as she soaked up the sun. "You're brave to lay here without a top."

"You think so? I was in France last summer and all the beaches there are topless, so it just seems natural to me. Besides, if you can take off your shirt, it would be sexist if I couldn't."

"Hey, no argument from me, you look beautiful."

She sat up, moved her hand to shade her eyes and looked at him. "Okay, take off your shirt and we'll be even." Her lips held a playful smirk.

He self-consciously pulled off his black t-shirt and she viewed his muscled hairy chest, eyes raking down to his belly button, the top of his shorts and below.

"See, doesn't that feel better?"

"My name is Bill."

"Lisa," she replied and kissed him lightly on both cheeks, her breasts casually touching his chest. "That's the way they do introductions in France." She laughed with sparkle in her blue eyes. It seemed like she was purposely teasing him. "I hope you're not eating meat. I'm a vegetarian."

"It's tuna, but I'm an unrepentant carnivore."

"Oh well, I won't hold that against you. Join me on the blanket. I have some wine."

"I haven't noticed you on the campus and I've been all over this place."

"I bet you don't go into the art building often. I hang out there painting and sculpting a lot, that's why it feels so good to be out in the sun."

They spent the afternoon together. Lisa told him she was from Manteca in the Central Valley. Her mom worked for Gallo Winery in Modesto and her dad managed a small almond and peach farm. They were very conservative Christians and did not understand Lisa's artistic side. She was a rebel, a crazy vegetarian and a feminist. She felt a freedom they could not understand. They thought the country was going to hell and if Lisa didn't repent and change her ways she would surely find herself in eternal damnation.

She had saved her money all of her life, any Christmas gift, any odd jobs, to pay for her trip to France. Lisa savored her personal pilgrimage. She spent two whole days in the Louvre. Paris had opened her eyes to the world beyond California's central valley.

Then she headed south through the wine country, looking at the castles on hills above the grapes. Seeing the French castles, she felt like fairy tales could come true. Moving south she came to the beaches of the Riviera, where she lay topless and free.

She cried for two weeks when she returned home to the dry, hot, flat valley. She felt like she had returned to the world of the fifties TV shows that were in just black and white. Finally, she left for college in Sonoma County where many hills were clothed in grape leaves, reminding her of Bordeaux.

She was alive again.

"How would you like to come to dinner with me? I can cook." Bill asked her hopefully.

She smiled at him, "Can you cook French?"

"The closest I can come is Italian. I have some jars of sauce that'll knock your socks off. I know, meatless."

"I would like that," she said, her soft voice caressing him.

Dinner led to chocolate flavored kisses in the bedroom. Bill finally got to explore the beautiful body he had been looking at all afternoon. He felt like he was exploring France, the lovely hills, the beautiful valleys, finally reaching the deep forest.

After making love, Lisa started to cry. "Did I hurt you?" Bill asked.

"No," she said as she whisked some wet blonde hairs away from her moist eyes.

"I'm very happy." She cuddled her firm young body next to his, holding him very tight.

*

"What do you think of Lisa?" Bill asked his

friends a few weeks later.

Laura and Don were back from classes and the three were sharing a joint and some beer in the living room. It had been two weeks since Bill and Lisa had started their romance.

Don captivated by her blonde good looks and bubbly personality said, "I think she's great. I think you've found yourself a winner."

Bill looked at Laura. "What do you think?"

She looked at him "Do you like her?"

"I think I more than like her."

"Do you really want to know what I think?"

"Yes."

Laura sighed. "She reminds me of my boyfriend, Joey. I think she may be bi-polar."

Bill knew the term from his nursing classes. He thought about it and shook his head. "Don't you like her?"

"Yes, I like her a lot. She's bright, beautiful and lots of fun, all the stuff that made me fall in love with Joe. But you've had to notice the mood swings. If you stay with her," she warned, "you're in for quite a ride."

The doorbell rang, interrupting the conversation. Don got up and opened the front door to Wilkes and a young lady standing next to him.

"You son of a bitch! What are you doing here? Guys it's Wilkes. Come in, come in." The old comrades hugged while the pretty athletic looking young lady watched with a smile.

"This is Joanie." Everybody went through introductions.

Bill said, "So how's the ski bum?" They knew Wilkes had been working at a ski resort near Truckee.

"I've been having the time of my life."

"What are you doing here?" Don asked.

"Everyone needs a break from skiing. I love it and I love Truckee. But the resorts are closing down. You might have heard that snow melts when the weather gets warm. Also I missed your ugly faces. Of course, Laura, I didn't mean you.

Laura laughed. "I see a newfound confidence in you, Wilkes. It's so cool. You look like a negative raccoon face all tan except around the eyes. Reminds me of the New York Wall Street crowd, in the winter, that went to Vermont for weekends in the mountains and came back faces all tan. Did you strike gold up there?"

"Well, I'm skiing almost every day and I met Joanie, my golden girl."

All eyes turned to the woman at Wilkes side. Her long legs were adorned in tight bell-bottomed jeans, a lavender sleeveless t-shirt with a shell necklace. Blonde hair was captured in a ponytail. She just smiled and waved shyly.

Wilkes grabbed her hand. "I love the Sierra. Worked all winter at the Alpine Mountain Resort, mostly as a lift operator, and skied almost every day. Next year they want to try me out as ski patrol, but I have to take first aid classes this summer.

"Anyway, here's the proposition, Joanie is from San Diego and I know Laura and Don have never been to Southern California. Do you guys want to do a spring break road trip?"

"Where would we stay?" Laura asked.

Joanie said, "No problem, my parents are

traveling to Europe. We can stay at our house in La Jolla."

"Can I bring my girlfriend?" Don asked.

Wilkes said, "That would be fine but with all the people someone else has to drive also."

Don asked, "If we have two cars caravanning, Bill do you want to bring Lisa?"

They looked at Joanie and she said, "The more the merrier."

Bill said, "I'll ask her. Let me see if Rick will watch Tilden or should I ask if he wants to come?"

"Whatever you want," Wilkes said.

"Can we make it down in one day?" Laura asked.

Joanie said, "It's a long drive, but possible especially if we take turns driving. I have the big jeep parked outside."

"Okay, it sounds like fun, but I have a lot of school work to do before spring break next week." Bill said.

"Could we crash here and explore for a week?" Wilkes asked.

Laura said, "Let's check with Rick, but I'm sure it would be alright. You two could have my room and I'll sleep on the fold-out couch."

"No way!" Wilkes said.

"Absolutely, I insist. That's the least I can do for my little brother's other best friend."

"Do you think Rick would want to go?" Don asked.

"I don't think so. I think he has a real estate deal, but I'll ask him when he gets home."

*

Spring break started and Saturday morning, after a quick breakfast in Cotati, the seven compatriots set out for San Diego in the two cars drove over the Richmond San Rafael Bridge, across the East Bay, to the Central Valley, joining interstate 5 to take them south. Laura rode in the Jeep with Wilkes and Joanie. Don drove the Cougar, Kathy riding shotgun while Bill and Lisa snuggled in the back seat. When they passed the exit to Manteca, Don asked Lisa if she wanted to stop and see her parents.

She frowned and said, "Hell no!" She looked out the window to the east where the peach orchards bloomed. Lisa sat, becoming quiet, tears in her eyes.

Bill asked, "You okay?"

"Those trees reminded me of growing up here. It is pretty in the spring when the peaches and almonds bloom. It's too bad my parents are such uptight assholes. I may never come back here again."

Bill kissed her on the forehead trying to take some pain away. Both his parents died while he was in Vietnam. His father, the alcoholic, had never recovered from the horrors being one of the few survivors when his ship sank from a Nazi submarine's torpedo in the North Atlantic. He finally succumbed to liver damage in 1970. His mother was despondent over his father's death. Bill's absence also took a toll. The resulting depression led the woman to take an overdose. He realized that Lisa's depression could be contagious, infecting his mood.

There were no cities, no towns, just exits with gas stations and fast food restaurants down Interstate 5 along the western side of the central valley. Don said to Kathy, "This reminds me of western Nebraska, long and flat."

They stopped at McDonald's somewhere southwest of Fresno. Lisa, the vegetarian, ordered a hamburger bun without the meat and an extra slice of tomato. Two hours later they went over the Grapevine, the pass over the San Gabriel Mountains and then quickly down to the megalopolis that was Los Angeles--a seemingly endless suburban sprawl. They headed to the 405 along the western edge of the city and got caught in the afternoon rush hour, inching along even on a Saturday.

"I wish I didn't have that second Coke. I have to tap a kidney." Bill squirmed in his seat.

"We may never make it to an exit. We're stopped on the freeway going nowhere," Kathy said.

"Shit. Just pass me the empty Coke cup." Bill proceeded to zip down his fly and peed into the cup. The traffic was still stopped when he opened the door and poured the contents on the asphalt of the fast lane. Finally, in the early evening, the Jeep and Cougar passed the enormous Camp Pendleton Marine

Base where Bill trained before Nam. He thought about the squad and all his buddies who didn't come home.

Lisa said, "You have a strange frown on your face. "Have you been here before?"

"Yeah," was all he said and she left it at that.

After the long day of travel, they were on the outskirts of San Diego and pulled up the long driveway to Joanie's childhood home.

*

As the three couples settled into the house, Laura disappeared, deciding to go for a long walk along the beach. She felt wonderful in the evening glow as her bare feet sifted through the cool sand. This was the California of her dreams on those cold winter nights in New York. The ocean views and endless surf made her play a symphony in her mind. The March evening was warm, yet she felt a chill as she looked out at the ocean. Laura thought she saw something big in the water close to the beach, but then it was gone. Was it a dolphin, a shark, a whale, or just her imagination? She had a strange premonition that something unique was going to happen on the beach tomorrow. She shook off the image and went back up to the house.

Sunset over the Pacific gave way to a twilight golden glow as the sun sank behind the fog cloud on the horizon. The seven visitors to Southern California were relaxing in the large living room looking out of a big picture window that faced the ocean. Eight thousand square feet of house nestled in the hills above the beach at La Jolla. From the outside, the house looked like a seventeenth century Spanish villa, red tile roof and stucco walls. Once you walked in the front door, the contrast was obvious: ultra-modern, very hip.

Bill shared a big chair with Lisa. She looked at the wall behind her and her mouth dropped open. "No fucking way! Is that a Jackson Pollock?"

Joanie shrugged. "I think so. My parents bought that from an art dealer in New York last year."

Lisa informed her friends that that painting was worth over a million dollars. Don walked over and looked closely at the paint splattered canvas.

"You're shitting me. It looks like something you put against the wall to keep paint from dripping on the floor."

Lisa laughed. "I know. I don't get him myself. But art is in the eye of the beholder."

Bill nodded his head and looked from the painting across from the view outside the big picture window. "No kidding. I'd rather look at that beautiful sunset. Maybe God's got his paint brush out. There is a saying at sea, 'Red sky at night sailor's delight.' So it probably won't rain tomorrow."

Lisa said, "I don't think you have to worry it almost never rains in Southern California this late in the spring."

Bill laughed, "Well I think we both jinxed it. Watch, it will pour." He turned to Lisa wrapped her in his arms, kissed the back of her neck again and again. She giggled and flinched in the reaction to the sensations from his kisses.

"That so tickles."

"Want me to stop."

"Never!"

Laura lay on a couch facing the window after her beach walk. "Nice digs, Joanie."

"What this thing? No big deal."

"What do your parents do?" Don asked.

Wilkes answered for her. "Her dad sells military equipment to the navy."

Lisa looked troubled. "Not bombs, I hope."

"It's just heavy equipment stuff," Joanie said. "My Dad and I have agreed not to talk about the war."

Wilkes, looked out the picture window, raised his glass of a cold salted margarita and said, "Now this is how I pictured California. I love skiing. But I always wanted to surf in the Pacific."

Laura said, "It's quite a beautiful sunset and the house is lovely. How did a So-Cal girl like you find herself in the high Sierra?"

Joanie sat back and relaxed in Wilkes' arms. "I've been either surfing or skiing since I was a little girl. I love both the beach and the slopes, and a lot of the skills are the same. It's easy to imagine waves becoming moguls."

"I can see why you love the beach." Don said as he gazed at the rainbow colors adrift above the waves. "I thought I might never get down to the California beaches. Finally here we are. Cue up the Beach Boys."

Bill stopped kissing Lisa's back long enough to say, "Don, not the Beach Boys they are so yesterday. How 'bout the Eagles if we are going with a So-Cal Band?"

Joanie said, "The Eagles it is." The hostess put a record on the turntable.

The music blasted from the speakers vibrating Mr. Pollock's creation on the wall. "Welcome to the Hotel California…"

*

Rick did have a real estate deal in the works. As a fulltime student and the owner of the Penngrove Ponderosa, he only dabbled part time in the business. But opportunity knocked in the name of Susan and Larry Johnson. Susan was the typical housewife of the fifties and early sixties, dropping out of college to raise a son and daughter. With her youngest child attending junior college Susan decided it was her turn to finish her education. She enrolled as a student at Sonoma State, finding a small apartment in Rohnert Park and coming home on weekends. Larry, earning a six figure income as a NASA engineer, totally supported his wife's ambition.

A week before Wilkes' arrival at the Ponderosa, Susan had invited the geology club members to her house in the growing Silicon Valley. Thirty-two students migrated to the expansive south Bay Area home.

It was there that Rick met Larry and the two men immediately became friends. As the party went on around them, the two sat in the den and exchanged life stories. Rick was fascinated with Larry's work with NASA at the Ames Laboratory in Mountain View. Larry picked Rick's brain about real estate in Sonoma County.

"I'm thinking of leaving NASA. I've saved and invested well. I'm interested in growing wine business and would like to find just the right property in Sonoma to start my own winery. Would you be willing to look for something special for me?"

"Sure." Rick said, biting at the bit for this opportunity. "What experience do you have in running a winery?"

"None, but I've been reading about it and I think California wine is going to take off like one of the rockets I've been working on. One of my coworkers, Jack, worked as a chemist at a winery in Bordeaux. He knows a little about French wine making and wants to invest with me."

"Are you looking for another investor?"

"Are you interested?"

"I just might be. But I would have to sell the Penngrove property and move to the land. As a geology project, I've been studying about soils that grow good wines. I can make it my senior project. To use a biological term, we could have a symbiotic relationship."

Susan broke in on their meeting. "Larry you've been hogging Rick long enough. Did you two know there is a party going on?"

Larry said, "I'm glad you came back here. Rick and I…"

"Honey I'll hear about it later, come on join the party. Rick everyone wants to know where you went to and I want you to meet my daughter, Alice. She's in her second year of junior college and wants to go to school in LA. I was hoping you could talk some sense into her. She is at the age where her Mom knows nothing."

The party was going strong. People gathered around the pool in the backyard. A group of geology students had formed a band and were belting out *Gloria* from Van Morrison.

Alice, not knowing any of the Sonoma group hid behind large sunglasses on the far side of the pool. She was in a lounge chair listening to the music and reading *Rolling Stone*. Susan pullede Rick by the hand and brought him to her daughter.

"Rick, this is Alice." Susan made the introductions and walked away. Rick was taken aback. Alice wore a skimpy red bikini, her long blonde hair falling over her naked shoulders. She was gorgeous. Alice tilted her dark glasses up, looked at him with stunning sapphire blue eyes and said, "You're kind of cute for an older guy. Have you been conspiring with my mom about me?

"Actually I've been in talking to your Dad. We may be doing business together."

"Oh, well if my Dad thinks you're okay, you must be doing something right."

"I must admit your mom wanted to talk you out of going to college in Southern California."

"Sorry but I've already got my heart set on USC. You know at some time you have to break away from your parents."

"Oh yeah I know that rebellion phase well."

"Why what did you do?"

"Dropped out of college to get married."

"See you know what I'm talking about."

"Yeah, now I'm divorced and back working to get my degree."

Alice laughed. "So I guess you showed them. Still, I'm not dropping out, just getting away. I need to be on my own."

"I understand," Rick said. "Listen I am going to go, I have some stuff to work on for your dad. It was nice meeting you."

"Too bad, I was just starting to like the party. Bye, Rick."

*

The San Diego spring morning invited the early surfers in wet suits out into the waves looking like seals. The mist retreated as the sun's rays attacked the beach. The tequila fog cleared much slower in the brains of six La Jolla companions. Only Laura, due to her night beach walk, escaped the hangover epidemic. Aspirin and coffee preceded the bacon, eggs and toast. They canceled a trip to Sea World and decided the beach, the sun, and the ocean was just what they needed. The group packed a picnic lunch, walked down to the beach, and spread blankets on the soft white sand. Bill jogged out to the water and dove into a wave while Lisa stood at the water's edge. "Damn, that water is cold!" Bill yelled.

"That's probably why those surfers are

wearing wet suits," Lisa laughed at her shivering boyfriend, bringing him a towel.

Lying in the sun on a blanket, Laura shivered also. She felt something was wrong. Her intuition pinged like a Geiger-counter near uranium. The uncomfortable feeling she had the night before returned. She sat up, looking at the sea and saw the fin in the water behind the surfers. It was too late to shout a warning to get out before she saw the great white take a bite.

"Oh God! Help me!" the injured surfer shouted. He tried to paddle on his board, pushed by his buddy. As the two approached the shore, Bill saw the large gash in the surfer's abdomen. His intestines were exposed, blood oozed from the deep wound. Only the wet suit and the cold of the water had kept the young man from bleeding to death.

Bill had seen this type of wound before, without teeth marks. His wartime medic training and experience took over. He tied his towel across the wound tightly while applying heavy pressure. Don ran up the trail to a phone booth to call for an ambulance.

Ten minutes later a helicopter was landing on the beach. A crowd of people had gathered to watch as the San Diego hospital Medevac team loaded the surfer onto the chopper, lifted into the sky, and flew away. The crowd dispersed and Bill returned from his flashback. As quickly as it happened, the beach seemed to return to normal. The helicopter sounds were replaced by the pounding of the waves.

Bill walked down the beach, away from the others. Laura turned to the visibly shaken Lisa and said, "You stay here. Okay?" Lisa nodded quietly as Joanie came to fetch her back to the blankets.

Laura walked down the beach towards Bill, where he was sitting on a big rock wall. She sat down, held his hand and he looked up at her with tears streaming down his face.

"Talk to me," Laura said to her friend.

Bill just shook his head and wiped the tears. "Just another day at the beach, huh?"

Laura wrapped her arms around him and held him for a minute, sharing her body's warmth in the cool early morning air.

"I'm okay now. I was back in Nam for a moment. It was the helicopter that did it. Freaked me out."

"I know. I saw that shark last night when I took a walk. It was close to the shore. I wasn't sure what it was but I know now I saw it."

Bill started laughing hysterically, relief coming to the surface with laughter, tears and snot. He tried to wipe his face.

"What's so funny?"

"You could have warned me before I went into the water."

*

Bill called the hospital. The surfer was out of surgery and stable. The hospital wanted his name to give him an award. He just hung up.

That night Laura and Don sat alone together in the family room. The brother and sister each had coffee, with good French cognac, the type they couldn't afford at school.

"Don, I had a premonition. I knew something

strange was going to happen."

"I wouldn't tell that to many people, they would just think you were crazy."

"Do you believe me?"

"Yeah, why not? You have always been intuitive. . . Uh, Laura, do you think we were there for a reason? If we weren't hung-over we would have been at Sea World. If Bill wasn't there that guy would be dead."

Laura looked up, thinking with a faraway look in her eyes. Finally she smiled and shrugged. "Just another mystery Bro. It's a strange wonderful world. The more we learn the less we know."

She pulled out a joint and said, "Here, let's explore this slightly different type of reality." Don laughed with his sister, reached for the joint, and they each took a hit of the green Northern California Sunshine.

Chapter 8

A Stunning Golden Eagle Day and
A Cold Foggy Manteca Winter Night

Rick drove Larry and Susan Johnson to the north end of Dry Creek Valley, to a small broken-down house that backed up against the redwood forest covered hillsides at the end of a long dirt driveway. Four hundred acres of Gravenstein apple orchard stood in front of the house.

Rick said, "The property includes all the apple

orchards and fifty acres of forest."

"Wow, this may be just what we're looking for. What do you think Larry?" Susan said.

"It's a beautiful piece of property. Is it in the price range we talked about?"

"Less, the owner wants to sell. His wife has passed and he no longer can take care of the orchards."

They went inside the old farmhouse. It looked even smaller on the inside, just three attached rooms with only a Franklin stove for heat. The small kitchen had an old gas stove that looked like an antique, only two burners and a black pipe going from the oven to the ceiling.

"This must be over a hundred years old," Larry said.

The fridge was an old ice box, small and square. They went back to the bedroom, where the paint peeled off the wall, and the smell of mold was pervasive.

"We would need to pull this down and start over," Larry said, as he put his finger against the rotting wood behind a bookshelf. It cracked from the pressure of his thumb.

Back outside, they walked the grounds as Rick continued, "The apple orchards still produce, but have been neglected. They could be replanted with grapes."

Susan said to her husband, "I think we have found it. This is the spot. It would take a great deal of work, but it's exactly what we want. I feel good about this land."

Rick said, "I think it's perfect for a winery. Not too far from the main road, where you could set up a wine-tasting center and we could even make a profit from the apples until they're replaced."

Larry pointed. "We could put the main house there and the winery over there, near the main road with the tasting room right behind it. Rick, have you picked out your spot?"

"Back there by the redwoods, I think."

Susan got excited. "Let's put in a bid."

Rick reminded the couple, "You know, I'm still a year away from selling the Penngrove property."

Behind the house, a trail carried them to the top of a hill. Larry viewed the whole property and beyond. "That's fine, Rick. We have the money for the property. Your investment will go to winery improvements, planting grapes, buying stainless steel and oak barrels. Let's draw up a contract. This is it. Put in a bid."

Rick agreed, "It's a beautiful valley and the hills are covered in redwoods. The soil samples I did show great wine potential. I think you guys are spot on. Dare I say it: Eureka!"

Susan had brought a bottle of wine and poured three glasses. Just then a golden eagle swooped down, snagged a small rabbit and flew off leaving three mouths agape. Susan was the first be able to find words. "Incredible! That was more than a sign. It's fate. To The Golden Eagle Winery!"

Rick and Larry nodded agreement held their glasses out to the amazing bird that soared out of sight as they drank.

*

After returning from the San Diego trip, Lisa invited Bill over to her small off-campus apartment for a romantic candle-lit dinner. She prepared Oysters Rockefeller made from fresh oysters grown in Tomales Bay.

"You know that oysters are supposed to make you more virile," she said in a sexy voice after kissing him hello and pinching his butt playfully. She had dressed in a black silk shirt, a short pleated skirt with a wide black belt and black high heels. Lisa kept referring to him as "my big hero," which made him feel uncomfortable. Still, he felt remarkably drawn to her when she was happy. She could give off a vibe as a prim school girl one minute, a centerfold belonging on the pages of Playboy the next, or morph into a moody bitchy woman that could drive even her best friends away.

Lisa showed him her best side as she grilled shrimp skewers for dinner and served them with a large salad and a cold mug of beer. After Bill wiped the foam from his mouth, she told him she had a surprise dessert for him but he had to go into the bedroom and take off all his clothes.

"Close your eyes," she yelled through the door.

He heard her come into the room, turn off the lights and light a match.

He smelled the aroma of an apple spice candle mixed with her perfume.

"Open your eyes." Her skirt was gone, her shapely body reflecting a dim glow. Lisa gave a seductive smile, clad in only her open inviting shirt, frilly black silk panties and matching stockings with high heels. "We are the desert."

In her left hand was can of whipped cream. She pressed the trigger and sprayed the sticky foam all over Bill's chest. Lisa advanced, her tongue dancing slowly to lick the cream. She stripped off her shirt, sprayed a dollop of cream on each nipple and with a snicker said, "Your turn."

*

When Bill called her two days later after class, she answered with a groggy voice. "Hello."

"Your dinner was so much fun the other night, thanks."

"What time is it?" she asked sounding as foggy and cold as a January Manteca night of her childhood.

"Didn't you go to class?"

"No, I didn't feel so good."

"Do you want me to come over and take care of you?"

"No, asshole! Do you think I need someone to take care of me?"

"Lisa, it's me. I'm on your side."

"Okay sweets, I'll call you tomorrow," and she hung up on him.

What the hell was that? He wondered.

*

Bill looked for Lisa at school the next few days. She didn't show up for classes. He called her place many times but there was no answer.

Friday at midnight, at the Ponderosa, Don was sitting in the living room cuddling with Kathy. They were watching Johnny Carson on *The Late Show* when the phone rang. Don got up to answer it. "Bill, it's for you."

Bill picked up the telephone and found Lisa on the other end. She said cheerfully, "What are you doing? Come over, sweetie."

"I've tried to call you for a week. Where have you been?"

"I had to take care of something."

"What?"

"Let's not get into that now. Come on over, I miss you. I've got cold beer in the fridge."

His mind had a quick debate. His libido won. "Okay I'll be over shortly."

When he got to her apartment, the lights were dark and candles were lit. She kissed him hard on the lips before he could ask any questions. Clothing was ripped off and left by the door. Passion took over.

As they cuddled blissfully, he started to ask Lisa about the last few days, when she put a finger on his lips and said, "Shush, let's not get into it. Just hold me tight."

When he awoke, he heard her in the kitchen.

Bill pulled on his underwear and walked up behind her. He saw her dressed only in her silk blouse.

"How do you want your eggs?"

"To hell with the eggs." He was hungry but not for eggs. He grabbed under her blouse and they made love right on the kitchen table.

After breakfast, as the bright sunlight came in through the window, he saw the telltale marks on the inside of her arm. He had seen those marks before, on the arms of squadron-mates in Vietnam. "Are you doing smack?"

Lisa looked shocked. "What are you talking about?"

He grabbed her arm roughly and held it up, the track marks facing both of them.

"You're not mad at me, are you?" She said sweetly in her most seductive voice.

"Lisa, I can't be with you if you shoot heroine. I'm serious. I can get you help."

"It's nothing. I've just done it a few times. It's not serious."

Bill had seen this act before. "Please let me

get you help."

"Fuck you! Who do you think you are? Get the fuck out of here!"

He looked at the beautiful woman in front of him, realizing that she was damaged, a beautiful porcelain doll with a little crack in it, just waiting to fracture down the middle. "I want to help you, but you have to meet me half way."

She laughed at him, the gorgeous face turning wicked, almost ugly. "Get the fuck outta here!"

So he left.

*

Bill had just taken a final in microbiotics and was standing outside the classroom when Rick walked up to him, a frown on his face.

"Rick, what are you doing here?"

"Bill, let's go get a cup of coffee."

"What's the matter Rick?"

Rick delayed for a second. He grabbed Bill by the arm and said, "Come on. Let's get outta here. Let's grab a cup of coffee."

"Just tell me."

"Lisa's dead. She overdosed."

Bill's knees buckled. The blood rushed from his face. What was wrong with him? He wondered. He could save a stranger, the surfer in San Diego, but he couldn't help his own girlfriend. He had this awful helpless feeling again... Like he had before....

Chapter 9

Sierra Days and Disco Nights

Don worked shirtless, laboring in the warm June sun. He noticed that he didn't sweat as much here as he did in the New York summer, yet he was thirstier in the dry California heat. He was part of a team building the main house for the winery property of Larry and Susan Johnson. The head contractor had hired a group of Mexican-American workers but Don desperately needed a job and Rick had hooked him up.

The Johnson's were thoroughly engaged in the project and worked along with their crew. They wanted to build a house by the end of the summer. They had sold their Silicon Valley property, Larry quit his job, and they moved to an apartment in Santa Rosa. Don commuted to work from the Ponderosa. His two years of high school Spanish, however rusty, became invaluable working with the Hispanic crew. Don, Susan, and Larry often had lunch together and were becoming good friends.

"Kathy is a doll. Is your relationship serious?" Susan asked Don.

"I guess so. We seem to fit together and well, it's easy. But we haven't talked about our future or anything. Why do you ask?"

Larry answered between bites of his ham and cheese sandwich, while taking sips of a Tab soda. "We have an offer for you that could change the relationship between you and Kathy."

Don put down his pastrami on rye and looked

at his employer. "What do you mean?"

"You're a great worker and we know that you've had two years of economics classes at Yale. You've told us that you're not sure psychology is the right major for you at Sonoma State. We know how smart you are and would like to pay for your senior year taking agribusiness classes at UC Davis. In other words, we want you to get in the wine business with a contract to work for us. You could come back here on weekends."

Don was shocked. He never expected anything like this. "How does Kathy come into the picture?"

Susan answered, "You would have to move to Davis and you could only see her on the weekends. But you would be working here. Kathy is one of my best friends in the geology department so if your relationship is serious, she could work here on the weekends with you."

"Wow, can I think about this, maybe talk to Kathy?"

"Of course, but we need an answer by the end

of July so we can get the paperwork in for you to start at Davis as our employee," Larry said.

Don looked at the redwoods and the apple orchards. He then looked at the young grapevines in the valley with a new appreciation. This valley was a beautiful place and he suddenly felt a part of it. He was awed by the proposal and the commitment it would take. "Thank you for offering this amazing opportunity. You know we really could do something special here." He realized that he had said "we."

*

Rick was relaxing over a self-made breakfast Saturday morning in early June. He had planned the day hanging out and relaxing. School was out, no papers due or tests to take. From the winery real estate deal, he was financially set for the summer.

The phone rang and he answered. "Hello"

"Hi Rick. This is Alice Johnson."

"Alice, you know, like Larry and Susan's daughter, Alice?"

"Guilty as charged."

"Did your parents want you to give me a

message?

"No, listen. I called to speak to you. I was up visiting my parents at the wine property. My mom brought up your name. Which made me think of how cute I think you are and wondered…if you're not busy…would you go to Stinson Beach with me.?"

"Are you asking me out?"

"Kinda…well yeah."

"How old are you? Didn't you just graduate from high school?"

"Two years ago, I'm twenty. Why do you just date older women?"

Rick was intrigued, she was so beautiful, but there was no way he would think about doing this if Susan hadn't brought them together to talk. But to call him at home was so brave. He knew how hard it was for a guy to ask a girl out. "I'll call you back in five minutes."

He dialed Susan's office number. She picked up. "Hello."

Rick asked, "Hi Susan, it's Rick. Is Alice at your winery property?"

"Yes, why?"

"She just called to ask me out."

"You want my permission? Rick please take her out. You should see the bunch of losers she has been hanging out with."

"Okay," Rick said. "If you're all right, I'll go."

"You better call the other number. If she knows I said it's okay she wouldn't go."

"Roger that."

Rick dialed the other number, Alice answered. "Rick?"

"Yes, It's a go. I've cleared my schedule."

"Great, be ready to go in a half hour. I'll pick you up."

He had never been asked out by a woman, but even for these days of women's lib this was strange.

*

Alice was a late baby-boomer feminist, aware, not ashamed of her sexuality. She knew men found her very attractive, came from a well to do family and always excelled in school. Self-confident, she had been a cheerleader until that bored her. She then preferred to hang around with Berkeley's artistic or musician types with no money and bad grooming habits. This was a much better idea and she even had the blessing of her parents. They liked the guy and he really was good looking.

*

Young Ms. Johnson picked Rick up at the Ponderosa. She drove her Mercedes 280SL convertible uncomfortably fast on the winding mountain road to the beach, a pink leather jacket with a faux fur collar over a white sundress. Her blond hair flew in the wind.

Rick threw on cut off jean shorts, a black Jefferson Airplane t-shirt, white running shoes, and a button-up jean jacket. Between the wind and the loud Steve Miller Band tape, they had to yell to be heard. So Rick kept quiet and held on tight to the door handle until they were safely past the cliffs and approaching Stinson Beach.

They parked the car, grabbed blankets, towels, and a large plastic cooler she had packed earlier. The two made their way to the north side of the beach below a cliff and behind a rock outcropping away from the wind and other people.

The big blanket was spread out and Alice slowly stripped off her jacket and sundress leaving only her skimpy red bikini. He only removed his jacket and shoes, knowing that he was unlikely to go into the cold churning northern California surf.

"So why did you call me?" The twenty-nine-year-old Rick asked the girl nine years his junior. Did you want to piss off your parents?"

"I told you, I think you're cute and smart. I figured you weren't going to call even if my parents approve. So I decided to do something about it."

"But there must be hundreds of young men closer to your age to go out with. What would you see in an older man like me?"

"The truth be told, you're confident, good looking and I'm tired of immature young boys. They are always in a hurry, if you know what I mean. Besides I am leaving for So Cal at the end of the summer, so let's have a good time."

She took his hand and brought it to her flimsy red bathing suit top. She smiled looking into his eyes then stole a kiss, like she was tasting wine then long and passionate, her tongue dancing in his mouth.

What the hell, he thought, in for a dime, in for a dollar.

Alice removed her suit and lay against a sleeping bag on the blanket. She put her hands behind her head pushed out her chest like she was proud to show off her body. He could tell she knew she could use her beauty as power to get what she wanted. Lying on the blanket naked, her silky light blonde hair and flawless golden skin, reminded him of a yellow rose in full bloom, unblemished petals almost perfection. Her floral perfume heightened the effect acting like a love potion… Dizzy from yearning, he hovered over her like humming bird that needed her life-sustaining nectar. Diving in to the folds of the flower he drank the honey like a lover until pollen plums burst. Bird and flower screamed together spent.

Alice, her pistil tantalized, was ready for round two. She grabbed a bottle of oil and rubbed every inch of his skin, recovered, he was ready to fly again.

After the second pollination, Rick surrendered. "You win. You are unbelievably insatiable."

The blood returned to her cheeks. She laughed, "How in the world…my goodness, that was awesome. You know every spot don't you…it was perfect except for the damned sand."

Rick said, "I've never dealt with anybody like you." The breeze washed over them as they lay below the wind, the golden sunshine warming their bodies.

"That's the first time I made love since my divorce."

"I think I like the idea of that Rick, kind of makes it even more special," she said, long fingernails scratching his hardened tan skin.

*

Bill sucked air, breathing hard, not acclimated to the altitude like his friend Wilkes. The Desolation Wilderness Trail switch-backs sent them on a steady climb up for the last hour. With almost fifty-pound packs and out of breath, the two men had to stop and take a break. Tilden also labored with a full pack that included his food and two plastic bowls. A cool spring flowed from a crack in the granite and the two guys pulled off their packs.

"Let me get that for you boy." Bill pulled off the dog's pack. They filled their aluminum Sierra cups in the spring bubbling up from the ground and drank deeply. The Sierra springs were so pure. Tilden lapped the water right from the rocks. Bill took a biscuit from Tilden's pack and gave it to his pet with a pat on the head.

"He's a great dog," Wilkes said.

"I know. He really seems to love it up here. I can see why you like it so much."

"You've been so quiet. How are you doing buddy?"

Bill shrugged his shoulders.

"Do you miss Lisa?"

"I don't feel like I knew her that well. It was almost like I was a moth attracted to a candlelight, or maybe she was the moth because she was the one that flew into the flame."

"Did you love her?"

"I was in love with her. She was so alive one moment, but as Laura warned me, the girl was a roller coaster ride. What about you, are you in love?"

"Absolutely, Joanie is the best thing that's happened to me. You should see her ski. She just floats like she's weightless."

"I'm happy for you, man. I see how your confidence has grown. I hear you learned how to ski really well last year."

"Well, I still have a long way to go if I want to be on ski patrol like Joanie."

While sitting, they took turns looking at the topographical map. "Looks like we only have one mile till camp," Bill said. "The alpine forest is so different from the redwoods. It's wide open up here. The views go on forever, sky so blue, sun so bright."

Wilkes looked at his buddy with a smirk on his face. "Man, you sound almost like a poet, maybe you could write some lyrics for Dylan."

"Yeah, right."

"Do you ever hear from Jenny? I thought you really liked her for a while."

"I did. Can one person fall in love twice in such a short while?"

"I guess you did. Or maybe it was just lust."

"I believe it was more than that. Maybe after Vietnam I was in love with the idea of falling in love. Anyway, I got my Dear John letter from her. You're not going to believe it but she met a Navy flyer. She is going to be the wife of Lieutenant Jefferson Thompson, USN."

"You're kidding."

"Nope, I guess she chose the military life style over us semi-hippies"

"Wow."

That evening they camped on the backside of Mount Tallac. The boys cooked macaroni and cheese over their campfire, adding beef jerky.

Bill asked, "Do you notice that a box of macaroni and cheese tastes better up here than a fancy restaurant dinner in Santa Rosa?"

"Yeah, well, I'm a lot hungrier and the view

ain't bad either."

Tilden gobbled up his dinner, then growled and started barking.

"What is it boy?" Bill asked.

"Over there in the trees, see it? Stay quiet."

A large brown bear looked at them, the smell of food obviously attracting her. Tilden stopped barking, then lay down and just looked at the bear growling. The bear did not move towards them or away.

"I've got this," Wilkes said and reached into his pack and pulled out a cap gun. Three shots into the air sent the brown bear scurrying away.

"Do you think she'll be back?" Bill asked.

"We need to take our food and tie it up in a tree. Make sure we take no food in our tent and I'll grab the cap gun just in case."

"Good, I think Tilden will let us know if that big bear comes back."

Bill put a sweater on Tilden before getting in his sleeping bag. The nights at nine thousand feet could get cold even in early July, but they certainly didn't expect the light blanket of white that greeted them in the morning. Snow was falling like it was January in New York. Yet as quickly as the summer storm appeared, it blew away. The late morning sun turned the white blanket of snow into a sheet of shinny mica speckled wet granite. They left the food up a branch of a big pine and headed for the tree line with just day packs.

The two friends walked up the trail switch-backing up to the peak of Mount Tallac. By noon the two buddies were sitting on the last remnants of the morning snow dusting the glacial peak. They looked down at the blue expanse of Lake Tahoe, with the finger of Fallen Leaf Lake and Emerald Bay right below them.

"Wow!" Bill marveled at the view.

"How are your flatlander lungs doing?" Wilkes asked.

"Fine, as a matter of fact, despite the thin air, I feel like I can breathe for the first time since Lisa died. I really needed this. Thanks for taking me here, Wilkes. You've turned into quite the mountain man."

"Ready to go down?"

They stood. Bill screamed and listened. No echo answered. Bill smiled and shrugged. "Worth a try." They took one last look at the incredible view and turned to head down the mountain.

As they hiked back to camp, Tilden stopped. The hair on his back stood up and he growled. Wilkes looked up to see the bear tearing into a big bag of trail mix.

"You son of a bitch!" he yelled. Wilkes took his cap gun and ran at the bear, pointing it at him and firing like it was a real gun. "That's my fucking food, you big asshole!" he yelled. Tilden ran behind him barking. The startled bear looked up in shock and took off, crossing the creek in one splash and running out into the woods.

Bill came running up behind Wilkes. "Are you out of your mind?" he said, more as a statement than a question.

"Well, I didn't think about it. I'm just hungry." The two men started laughing until tears ran down their cheeks.

The bear had snapped the small branch holding their food, tore apart the stuff bag containing their food and all that was left was part of a box of Rice-a-Roni.

"Well, we sure showed him." Bill said. "At least we've still got some of the San Francisco treat." They started laughing again. They cooked what was left of the Rice-a-Roni over a fire for lunch, took down their tent and started down the mountain.

*

"So where are we going?" Rick asked Alice as she drove through North Beach in San Francisco. She was dressed in a short black minidress showing lots of cleavage and black platform high heels. Two gold chains around her neck completed her mod-disco look. She had told him to dress nicely, so he had to dispense with his faded bell bottom jeans, wearing instead a pair of gray slacks, a white shirt, and a black thin tie from his real estate days. He covered it all in a black leather jacket. When he had walked in the door, Alice said, "You look nice, but lose the tie, too uptight."

"We have reservations at Chez Nouveau, then dancing. Is that okay Rick?"

He was not into fancy French food. Rick was more or a steak and potatoes man, but he did want to please her, "Sounds good."

Dinner was sweet, dark, romantic. They shared a bottle of Alexander Valley Chardonnay. She had a false ID that claimed she was twent-two, not that the waiter asked. The lady was served scallops and the gentleman ordered a tiny undercooked piece of filet mignon with something drizzled on top so it could look pretty. The waiter completed the ambiance with his phony French accent. Rick yearned for a big overcooked almost-burnt hamburger and fries, leaving the restaurant with a still-hearty appetite.

Alice handed him the keys and slid into the passenger seat, pulling on the hem of her minidress to try, unsuccessfully, to keep it from riding up to her black lace underwear. Rick tried to keep his eyes on the road as she gave directions.

Rick realized the rest of the night would not

go well when he saw the bouncer out in front of the night club dressed in an orange wide-lapel shirt and a blue leisure suit. He pulled back the fuzzy velour black rope to let her in but shook his head at Rick until she said, "He's with me."

The drumbeat pounded and black light made the wall glow as the big disco ball turned. Rick thought, Oh no. How does a rock n' roll guy live in this disco world?

Alice grabbed his hand and pulled him to a table in the back of the big room, introducing him to three of her girlfriends. He knew she was showing him off as the other disco dolls checked him out to see what Alice had on her dinner plate.

"Oh, my word, are you two an item yet?" Lynn, the brunette with a gold L above her low-cut red dress asked. She already knew the gossip but had to pose the question to make conversation.

"Come on, let's dance." Alice pulled Rick out under the disco ball as the electronic sound track pounded behind soul vocals. The prefab dance tunes blared out from the large speakers on the glowing wall. Rick was definitely not little Stevie Wonder. He had his one white boy move of the fist pump and a stomp. Alice floated around him light on her feet, even with those huge disco clomper-heels. She laughed playfully at his discomfort. She noticed the other men around the room watching. She did her best bump and grind. After all, the disco dance floor was for showing off your goods.

As the song changed, Alice kept dancing, her misty skin aglow under the lights as she heated up. Rick felt enough was enough, reached out and pulled her from the floor. Where could he take her? "Is there a quiet room in here?"

She pulled him into the girl's bathroom. Women were touching up their makeup, looking in the big mirror. They ignored the fact that a man just walked into their bathroom. Alice pulled him into an empty stall and kissed him. She reached into her tiny over-the-shoulder bag and pulled out a glass vial containing the telltale white powder, cocaine. She took out a small coke spoon, filled it and said, "Want some?"

"No thanks, I'm good." His thoughts went back to Lisa's overdose. Alice filled one spoon and snorted the white powder up her left nostril, then followed the same procedure for the right one. Her whole body shook and she said, "Come on, let's go dance."

"Alice, this really isn't my thing. You stay, have a good time, I'll catch a cab."

"Rick, stay please. I just want to dance a little. Then we can go back to my place. The sex is really good on cocaine." She gave him a pouty spoiled-child look.

Her beauty beckoned like a golden nugget to a 49er. Rick took one last good look at her beguiling face, like he was capturing a picture. He already knew this wasn't going to work. "I'll call you tomorrow, have a good time."

The cab dropped him at his car near the restaurant. He drove back to the Ponderosa, sad the romance was over. What seemed so sweet on the beach was so wrong in the disco.

The next day, they talked on the phone.

"Alice, you're wonderful, but this isn't going to work out."

"I'm transferring to USC at the end of the summer. We could just have a fun summer love affair, like in the movies."

"What movie would that be?"

She giggled, "I don't know."

Rick thought for a minute, tempted. "No, I think it's time to move on."

He could almost see her pout on the other end of the phone. "Okay, Rick, it was fun while it lasted."

Chapter 10
Dangerous Cliffs

Esalen Institute at Big Sur is a world famous center of humanistic psychology. Laura's Master's committee chairman, Dr. Tim Prescott, arranged to have her intern at the Institute as a job. She would learn firsthand from famous psychologists from all around the world. In exchange for room and board, Laura worked in the kitchen, giving her time to explore the redwood forest or the coastal beaches.

The cliffs of the Los Padres Wilderness battle

the Pacific Ocean for supremacy, resulting in an amazing, almost sacred natural wonderland. The goddess Pele had reached out and touched Big Sur, tectonic hot springs bubbled up through the canyons. One spring runs through Esalen and students and staff could relax and meditate in a large communal hot tub overlooking the ocean.

Laura lay back in her birthday suit in the hot water of the natural spring, enjoying the ocean view and the company of the other uninhibited bathers. As the late August sun fell for the night, the Pacific surf swallowed it, spitting colors of the rainbow across the horizon.

Dr. Phillip Grant was reviewing the Gestalt technique of the empty chair with Laura. She had watched as a group member talked to his dead mother using the method during an afternoon group session. Tears streamed down the man's eyes as he said things to her that he never was able to say when she was alive.

"So you see we learn about our innermost feelings. Accepting the image of the person in the empty chair, we learn to accept ourselves." Doctor Grant told Laura.

"I understand, I'm just amazed how powerful it is as a tool."

Seven people from different parts of the globe and generations were sitting in the hot tub, comfortable in their nakedness. Dr. Grant was from Baltimore, a sixtyish Buddhist monk came from India, a young blonde woman from Germany, a California couple in their fifties, a wealthy artist about thirty from Sedona, Arizona, and twenty three-year-old Laura from Sonoma County by way of New York.

"Laura, do you want to lead the group tomorrow?"

"Do you think I'm ready?"

"I think you're a natural. I'll be there to help you if you run into any problems. You are going to be a great therapist," Dr. Grant assured her.

She smiled. Confidence had never been a problem for her, but it had been a long, strange year. The conflict with her parents, the suicide of her boyfriend, the overdose of her friend Lisa, and the move across the country had taken a toll on her effervescent nature but as she felt the hot spring bubbles work their magic, she became so relaxed, one with the world.

*

The Big Sur summers run cold. Fog sits over the sea and invades the coast all summer, driving the sun inland and causing winds to blow from the ocean. In September, the fog retreats and the warming sun beats down on the land causing a budding bloom of autumn flowers on the coastal cliffs. On this beautiful morning the sun poured its warmth on the compound, reminding Laura that autumn was saying hello. It was time to return to school and her newfound family at the Penngrove Ponderosa. She had been offered a ride all the way to the San Francisco Airport, but turned it down. Laura wanted to walk along Highway 1, the coastal road, for a while, eating fruit from the ripened blackberry bushes and strolling through the redwoods one last time.

The young woman had been walking for a few

hours, her backpack comfortably containing her things, when she decided it was time to put out her blackberry-stained thumb to hitch a ride.

Only five vehicles had passed when a blue Ford pickup truck pulled over and the middle-aged driver said, "Hop in." The passenger door creaked as she opened it like it needed oil. Her intuitive sense told her something was wrong but she was too relaxed and too far from her New York street smarts. She threw her backpack in the back of the truck and slid into the passenger seat. "Where you goin' honey?" the man asked.

"Up north, Sonoma County."

"I can take you as far as Carmel. Just sit back and enjoy the ride. Sorry the radio don't work. You can call me Jack."

"That's okay…um Jack."

She was disappointed when she realized the right side of the truck faced away from the ocean and its spectacular view.

The pickup truck accelerated and braked through every curve, crossing a bridge over the beach gorge and then back to the cliff curves. The man stayed quiet and Laura followed his example. He was dressed in straight-legged jeans, white t-shirt, white socks and penny loafers without a penny.

There was a traffic light at the Safeway parking lot just south of Carmel. Jack pulled off, saying he wanted to get something at the store; but went right past the supermarket and turned onto a quiet street that dead ended into a dirt road.

"Where the hell are you going?" Laura asked, unnerved by the sudden route change.

He didn't answer, just kept driving. Laura pulled off her seatbelt and tried to jump out of the moving car but the door was locked. He accelerated down the dirt road for another quarter of a mile and then skidded to a stop in a wooded area. Laura went into survival mode and punched at his face but she only landed a glancing blow. He punched her back full on her jaw, almost causing her to black out. She shook her head and reached out to scratch his face as adrenaline exploded throughout her body.

Only then did she see his big buck knife. Jack

held the knife to her throat and said, "I would hate to hurt you, sweetie, so stop your struggling. Now I'm gonna get out of the truck and you follow me out the side. You got it? If you scream I'll cut your pretty head right off."

Laura was terrified but slid across the bench seat and out his door as he demanded.

He held the knife point against her ribs and said, "lay face down on the ground over there."

"What are you going to do?" she asked.

"Don't worry your pretty little head about it. Just lay down!"

"No, fuck you!" She yelled. Then he hit her hard and she fell to her knees. He hit her again and she felt her face swell below her eye.

She was face down on the cold wet leaves and the man took his sharp knife and cut off her clothing, pulled them off roughly and discarded them by the road. The knife nicked her back, causing blood to flow. She felt dizzy and nauseous.

Laura had trouble breathing and sucked for air, blood covering her lower back. He grunted like a pig when he entered her from behind.

"No!" she yelled and screamed to the empty road. The rapist pawed at her like an animal. She meditated and flashed back to her acid trip and focused on the ants crossing the dirt road. Laura distantly heard the pick-up truck start. The man was gone. She was still alive.

What was left of her clothing was filthy and bloody. Laura stood up groggily. She was wet inside and realized he had deposited his sperm. She vomited into the bushes. It was hard to see out of her left eye, her face felt hot and numb at the same time. Naked, she stumbled down the dirt road toward the Safeway.

She made it to the supermarket parking lot. People stopped and stared. A woman stopped loading her groceries, grabbed a blanket from the back of her Volvo and ran to her. As the blanket covered her body, Laura passed out.

When the police called the Ponderosa, Don, Rick, and Bill immediately drove to Monterey to get her. Rick had placed a rifle in the car announcing, "If I find that motherfucker I'll kill him."

Taken to the hospital, the police ran a rape kit, then interviewed her for two hours at the station. She was brave through it all, answering each question, holding ice packs to her face. Her backpack was found on the side of the road off Highway 1, but it was needed for evidence, so they gave her a prison jumpsuit until the boys arrived with her clothing.

*

"Bill, how do you do it?" Laura asked.

"Do what?"

"Put it behind you. The death, the combat, the killing, the blood, body parts, Lisa..."

"I don't have any answers for you. It's hard but you know what they say, what doesn't kill you makes you stronger."

Laura was wrapped in a blanket in the living room. It was a beautiful ninety degree day outside, in the sunshine, but she hugged the blanket like she was Linus in the *Peanuts* comic strip. Bill looked Laura. Her face was returning to its natural beauty after weeks of deformity. The swelling had gone down, yet a black eye remained. She looked too thin, like she was not eating.

Turning back to Bill, she said, "Really? That's the best you can do? 'What doesn't kill you makes you stronger,' what are you doing fuckin' reading me a bumper sticker?"

He ignored her hostility. She deserved his patience. "Laura, I just had to leave it behind. I still dream about the horror, sometimes have nightmares, but it gets easier further in the rear-view mirror."

Laura had a faraway look in her eye for a second. Then she came back and started to cry.

"Do you need a hug?"

"Please, yes." He sat on the couch with her and held her as she cried, her whole body shaking. Then she stopped, wiped her eyes and said, "Ok, rear-view mirror, doesn't kill you makes you stronger. I can do this."

"Are you going to start school next week?"

"Oh yeah, that motherfucker's not going to ruin my life."

"That a girl."

Chapter 11
Thou Shall Not Covet

As school started, Don was moving into the dorms at Davis and a new roommate was moving into the Ponderosa. Summer Darby was a geology major student friend of Rick's who grew up in Palo Alto.

Like many Californians, she was a mutt. Her Mexican mother, Maria Garcia, came alone across the border as a teen. At first she picked fruit, then she was hired as a housekeeper for a Stanford professor.

Summer's Irish-American father came to the Golden State from Boston during World War II. Hired as a dockworker, it was his first full-time job in two years. Tim Darby was one of millions of unemployed or underemployed during the Depression. His boss had learned he graduated from Boston University and moved him to an office in Menlo Park where he tested and designed wartime aircraft. Tim Darby was promoted after the war to become part of the new postwar aerospace industry. He met his wife in a Catholic church at a friend's wedding.

Summer made the best homemade tortillas and her Mexican food was the best her roommates ever tasted. Pretty and slightly plump, she had an infectious laugh and a great sense of humor. She played a practical joke on Rick once, leaving a harmless snake in his bed. He screamed like his pants were on fire. It made Laura's day. The two became close friends, allies in the friendly rivalry with the testosterone-driven boys.

All four were home in the early October evening when the phone rang and Rick answered it. "Laura, it's for you, the police."

Laura yelled, "I'll get it in my room." She went in, closed the door and picked up the princess phone next to her bed. The three others waited in silence just beyond the door, hoping to hear something. They could only hear her say, "yes, oh no. . . uh huh. . . yeah. . . holy crap. . . okay. . . . goodbye."

Laura came out of her room a few minutes later, sat down with a shocked look on her face. "They found the goddamned son of a bitch. He was in his pickup truck, dead. He lived in San Luis Obispo, raped a Cal Poly girl last March who saw him going into a bar last night. The girl went home, got her boyfriend who waited till he left the bar, then walked up and tapped on his driver's side window. He shot the asshole in the head as he rolled it down. The fucker's actually dead!"

Rick asked, "Are you okay?"

"How the hell do I know?"

Summer got up, went to her new friend, kissed her on the cheek, and said, "Here, put your head in my lap." Summer stroked Laura's hair. Laura cried for a while, then stood up and said, "Fuck him. He's not going to hurt anyone again. Good fucking riddance! I can move on with my life now."

*

Just south of Penngrove was the north Petaluma freeway exit. The Windmill Cafe and Motel stood under a fake Dutch-style windmill. Bill and his friend Ned were at the cafe having a late lunch. Bill paid the check and walked out to the parking lot, where he was shocked to see Laura kissing Professor Langston as they came out of a motel room.

Langston was a young, popular psychology professor with a wife and two children. Bill stopped in mid-step and stared, mouth dropping. Out of the corner of her eye, Laura saw Bill. Even across the lot he could see her face turn scarlet. Langston looked around, saw Bill and Ned without recognition and went to kiss Laura one last time. She turned her head, pushed him away and said her goodbyes. Bill said goodbye to Ned and drove back to the University for a class.

Back at home, Bill noticed Laura hid in her room, door closed with the radio tuned loud to KFRE, a rock station in San Francisco. Summer and Rick were out. Bill went to the kitchen, took his anatomy book out and tried to study, images of Laura and John Langston running through his mind. After about an hour his housemate emerged, marijuana smoke following her out of her room.

She sat in the chair facing him, "I suppose you want an explanation."

He shrugged. "You don't owe me an explanation, but do you really want to be with a married man?"

"Fuck it, Bill, I'm not married, he is. I'm free to do what I please."

"But Laura, he is married with two boys at home. Do you want to…"

"Maybe I do!" she screamed at him, "Men are such assholes. He deserves whatever happens to him. The fucker has made a million passes at me and other girls since I first took a class from him."

"So this is payback to the male gender."

"Only the assholes."

"What about his wife, what does she deserve?"

Laura broke down crying, "I don't know Bill, what the fuck I'm doing. You know I don't want to hurt anyone."

Suddenly she stopped crying, an awareness showing on her face. "His being married was safe. I wasn't with him to break up his marriage, but to take my sexuality back. It was dangerous for him but I knew he couldn't hurt me. I had all the power. Oh my god, holy shit."

"That's heavy holy shit."

"I know. But am I becoming one of them?" Her awareness came slowly. "I can't be another asshole. I need to be good to win against the bad. I need to be so much better than this."

Laura kissed Bill on the cheek. They were like brother and sister. "Where would I be without you? You're like my conscience, a regular fuckin' Jiminy Cricket."

Bill said, "There's an outpatient clinic in Santa Rosa. I've been offered a part time job there and to work after graduation as a nurse. They desperately need social workers. A lot of the vets

have post-traumatic stress syndrome. I think you have
it from the rape."

Laura looked at him intrigued. Suddenly a
smile appeared on her face. "Whatever doesn't kill
you makes you stronger. Bill, it was my fate… to
make me stronger so I could work with others."

*

That night Laura knocked on Rick's room
door. "Come in," he said.

She opened the door. He was sitting at his
desk reading a book. He squinted at her. "You okay
Laura?"

She didn't answer, walked over, pulled him
out of the chair and gave him a hug. Wrapped in her
arms he looked down at her, his eyes questioning. She
kissed him lightly just touching his lips. "I love you. I
mean I really love you. I have from the moment I met
you and I never told you. But life is too short."

Rick knew he was in love with Laura since the
rape. When he placed the gun in the car and
threatened to kill the guy. He never had that kind of

passion about anything or anyone before, certainly not for his ex-wife. He realized he was in love with Laura but how could he burden her with that after what she had gone through. They were housemates; he couldn't just make a pass and destroy their friendship. It was too important. She had always been off limits. Now here she was in his arms. He felt like the luckiest man in the world. He kissed her.

She loved him. If he only knew…he loved her from the moment she walked into the Ponderosa and changed his life. She was what made him what he was today. She made him part of this amazing family. He looked at her anew. She was so freakin' far out.

They kissed again with a craving that had been smoldering for a long time. The fire ignited. He explored her mouth with his tongue. He caressed every inch of her body, her face, her breasts, his fingers played along her abdomen running up and down her long legs. He wanted to be consumed wrapped inside her body like Spanish moss, plant and fungi living together as one being in symbiosis.

Laura responded with love and need,

touching him everywhere; he felt her reaching into his heart and soul. Her orgasmic scream echoed into his inner core and became part of him.

Laura said, stroking his sandy-colored hair. "That was my first orgasm since Joe's death on that cold winter day in Greenwich Village. I feel whole." He was amazed and delighted. Two had become one.

"I love you Laura."

Chapter 12
Thanksgiving

The early November morning dawned like the one before it, with clear blue skies and a cool mist that quickly burned off the brown hillsides. Laura looked out the window of the Ponderosa to see the horses romping on another beautiful day. The summer season refused to give way to winter, holding back the rains that replenished the state and turned the golden brown hills to green. To the north in Washington and Oregon the clouds were building, pregnant with water for a storm due to arrive tomorrow.

Since that first amazing night of love with Rick, Laura felt whole, free, and happy but her cycle was very late. She knew she was pregnant, felt it. How could she tell Rick? How would he react? What would she do with the child? She wanted to go to her friend, Summer, and ask her what to do. No, that was a copout.

Rick walked in the front door, yelled to Laura, "I'm home." He came over and kissed her. She didn't kiss back, just pecked with her lips. He knew something was not right.

"What's wrong?" He grabbed her hand. She turned away unable to face him. Finally, Laura decided to face the music. "I'm. . . I'm pregnant."

He did the math quickly in his head: mid-September, October. "It's his isn't it?"

The blood drained from her face. "Yes."

"What do you want to do?"

"Would you stay with me if I kept it?"

His face showed his shock. They hadn't yet talked about children and they had been careful in their love-making. After a few minutes of silence he said, "If that's what you want, I'm in. I love you."

She smiled, the cloud lifted. Laura made up

her mind instantly, when she had a child it would be Rick's, not that rapist's. "Will you go with me, take care of it…go to the abortion clinic?"

"Just name the time."

Laura took his hand and led him back to the bedroom. She loved her man more than ever.

*

The rain came the next day in torrents that fell on Sonoma county sending rivulets of water down the canyons and gullies. No amount of raingear could keep Bill dry on his bike ride from school. It seemed like the rain soaked not just his skin but his soul. His mental battle scars included the horrors of war and watching friends die including Tom, Lisa, Laura's rape. Now Tom's wife, Jill was dead.

Bill's mind flashed back to Da Nang, January 13, 1970. Marine Private First Class Tom Morgan was his best friend in the squad. The two were simply walking down the street when an unseen VC rolled a grenade behind Tom. The explosion knocked Bill off his feet but after a quick check he realized he was unharmed. Not Tom. The explosion opened a large gash across his back. Tom's blood was everywhere. Bill felt panic but ran over and applied pressure to the wound. He knew it was futile. Tom's wound was too big and he had lost too much blood. Bill was devastated; all his training could not save Tom. He shouted for help and a military ambulance arrived in minutes.

The scene played out in his mind like it was yesterday.

*

Bill had met Jill just before he and Tom were shipped out to Nam. Their river boat patrol squadron of sailors and marines had trained at Camp Pendleton, and then were given a week's leave in San Diego. Jill had flown out from New Jersey, toddler Tina in tow to say goodbye. Tom had told Bill their story.

Tom and Jill had been high school sweethearts. Tom, the orphan bad boy, lived with any relative that would take him. Jill was the cheerleader and honors student. They dated secretly for a while but when she got pregnant her parents wanted to send her away to get a quiet abortion. She split, left home.

Jill and Tom eloped and he joined the Marines to make ends meet. He went to boot camp, leaving her disowned by her parents and alone with the new baby in an apartment. They desperately missed each other.

After boot camp he was given two glorious weeks of leave with his wife and baby, but then his orders came sending him to Pendleton to train with the squadron going to Vietnam. She was being left behind as he readied for deployment. Tom sent her the money to come to San Diego. Bill went with him to the airport.

Jill stood out in the crowd of people disembarking from the plane. Her flaming red hair was teased up, flying like a great flag above an angelic face. When she saw Tom her emerald eyes came alive and her smile beamed. She grabbed Tina and beelined to Tom, they embraced kissing 'til out of breath, Tina shyly holding on to her mother's leg.

Bill noticed that the little girl resembled her mom, red-topped and freckled.

Jill said, "Do you remember your daddy?"

The word came out of Tina's mouth for the

first time as a question, "Daddy?"

Tom scooped her up as if she was weightless, held her over his head and said, "Yes I'm your Daddy and I love you so very much."

Tina still looked confused until Jill came over and hugged her and Tom, together. Tina giggled and planted her thumb in her smiling lips. Bill was introduced and the four went to dinner together.

Bill spent a lot of the week with the three of them. Tom and Jill loved that he volunteered to baby sit when they wanted to be alone. Bill loved his time with Tina. He almost felt like part of the family, Tina's big uncle. The beach, sightseeing, the week flew by faster than a marine fighter jet. Bill did not accompany them back to the airport when Jill and Tina left. He figured watching that sad scene was beyond the call of duty.

*

Even when he was broke he found a way to send Tom's wife and child some money back in New Jersey. They wrote to each other often, but Bill thought it would be too painful to see them without

Tom. Then just a few weeks earlier, Jill caught the flu and her temperature spiked quickly. It turned into viral pneumonia and ravaged her body like a wildfire. Inexplicably, she died in less than 14 short days. Tina was orphaned, alone. Tom and Jill named him her godfather, and Jill having no one else, put him down as the next of kin on her hospital papers. When the social worker called him and explained the situation, he knew what he had to do. Tina was his responsibility.

The Penngrove roommates gathered that evening and Bill explained the situation in the living room. They all pledged support for their beleaguered friend. The pain was visible on his face as Bill told them, "I want to bring her back here. How would you guys feel about that?"

Rick took the lead. "Bill, I'm here for you, if there's anything I can do. . ."

Laura had not cried for her aborted fetus, but she could not hold back the tears for her housemate and the abandoned little girl. "I'll move into Rick's room and Tina can have mine. I'll fix it all up."

Summer added, "I'll do any babysitting you need. I can't wait to meet her."

Bill looked at the three of them, his eyes red and shock still registering on his face. "She was just a baby the last time I saw her with Tom. She is six now, walking and talking, in first grade." He was telling himself as well as them. "Oh, I have to register her for school."

Laura said, "Send us the paperwork. I'll take care of it."

"Thanks, my flight leaves early tomorrow. I guess…" He couldn't finish the sentence before he broke down.

*

Bill arrived with little Tina in his arms. She had her arms wrapped around him like she was holding on for dear life. Her bright red dress matched her flowing fiery hair that extended half way down her back. Six-year-old Tina looked out at her new family with sparkling green eyes, freckled rosy cheeks and a button of a nose.

*

When Bill checked in at the agency to pick up Tina, she looked at him curiously, somehow remembering him from their brief encounter years earlier. "Daddy?" she asked, her memory clouded from the encounter with the two men in San Diego. He had spent more time with her then Tom.

"I'm your Uncle Bill and I am taking you to your new home."

"I want my mommy and my daddy!" She yelled and stomped.

Bill thought for a minute, then said, "It's okay Tina I'm your new daddy." He scooped her up like Tom did at the airport and held her over his head, and then dropped her into to his strong arms and she held on tight.

"Where's Mommy?"

"She had to go away," Bill answered, "but she misses you very much." That seemed to satisfy her for the moment. He sent her off to play with the other kids as he signed paperwork.

*

Laura and Summer indeed transformed Tina's new room: a fresh coat of paint was on the wall, a sleeping beauty comforter covered the bed, a teddy bear sat on top. Laura felt like there was some karma working with the young child coming into her life. She made a point of saying to the little Tina, "I'm your Auntie Laura. If there's anything you need, just ask."

It was Summer who just seemed to know what the child needed. When she heard Tina crying that night, she crawled into bed with her and stroked her hair. "It's going to be all right, darling." Tina fell asleep in her arms.

Tilden suddenly wanted to be very protective. He rarely barked before, but when Bill brought Tina into the house, he camped, out guarding the front door and loudly barked at anybody's arrival.

The Tuesday before Thanksgiving was a clear and crisp Sonoma day. Laura saddled her horse, Chardonnay, placed Tina in front of her so she could grab the saddle horn and cantered down the country road. Tina's eyes got as big as goose eggs. "Auntie

Laura this is fun. Go faster." Laura laughed, and with Tina safely tucked in her arms, made a clicking sound and Chardonnay took off galloping down the road.

*

"So, should I carve the turkey?" Rick asked.

Summer said, "Maybe we should say a prayer."

Bill turned down the stereo which was playing Simon and Garfunkel's *Bridge Over Troubled Water*. He looked at the multitude of friends around the table, Don, Kathy, Laura, Rick, Wilkes, Joanie, Summer and, of course, his new daughter, Tina. They were all part of his family now. "Thank you Lord for bringing Tina to our house and for the fellowship that we have here today."

"Amen"

"Can we eat now?" Tina asked.

Chapter 13
Beyond the Golden Gate

The geology club's Christmas party took place during the second week of December before the students went home for the holidays. The club had evolved to be more than just classmates. Many of them had become close friends. The group took a nickname they also used as the name of their club's softball team, Richter's Radicals.

The Ponderosa family was invited to the club's party at the new Golden Eagle Winery. The fertile land of the farm had been transformed. Rows of grapevines replaced the under-producing orchards of older apple trees to become grapes that would, in the near future, produce award-winning wines. The old farmhouse had vanished, replaced with a Tuscan style villa of glass, stucco, and redwood, under a red clay tile roof. It opened to a Greek-columned large center courtyard with a Roman fountain. A swimming pool was located behind the house, fenced in below redwood trees and covered for the winter.

The separate winery building, with a tasting room, sat on the opposite side of the farm, near the road, under the hill still partially covered by the naked winter branches of apple trees. Redwoods lined the road between the winery and the new house. It was a spectacular estate, pregnant with promise.

When Larry could separate Rick's hand from Laura, the two retreated from the party to talk.

"Susan and I have been talking. We want you to manage the marketing of the winery."

"I'm not qualified."

"Are you kidding? You had a successful real estate business. Susan knows you from classes, thinks the world of you. Then there's your great relationship with Don, our vineyard expert. Lastly, there is your significant investment."

"You know I don't have any experience with wineries."

"Unless you're Robert Mondavi or the Gallos, you probably have about as much experience as any Californian on to how to sell wine. We can hire consultants, but I know we can do this together. Plus we still need your knowledge of the soil."

"Thank you for the opportunity. It sounds great."

"Good, let's go back to the party."

Don, Kathy and Susan were back in the kitchen when Rick and Larry joined them.

Don said, "I'm glad to have you together," looking at Larry and Susan. "I want to thank you for giving me this opportunity to learn and work for you."

"We believe in you," Susan replied.

"As soon as I started in the viticulture department, I was captivated. When I was in the economics department at Yale, it all had no meaning. I couldn't see how I fit in. The psych department at Sonoma was interesting but I knew I didn't belong. Being there at Davis to learn how to help you with the wine business, I'm inspired. So I have a proposition for you. My dad and I have reconciled, he believes in what I'm doing. You remember I told you he is a brokerage house executive? He and I have been going over the numbers and if you go public, we believe you can be a year or two ahead in your goals. You can buy grapes from other vineyards until your grapes are ready. You can get more oak and stainless steel barrels and complete the winemaking capabilities without going into debt."

"I don't want to sell control of this place to get corporate investment," Larry said emphatically.

Don said, "No, there's no need for that. This would be a limited sale. You and Susan would stay in control with fifty-one percent and the other investors, like Rick getting maybe ten percent."

Larry looked at Don thoughtfully. "Can you guarantee we would not lose control?"

"Yes absolutely."

"Let's get our lawyer to look at this. Okay with you Susan?"

She nodded. "I'll let our guys go over this and I'll let you know what I think."

Kathy came into the kitchen, a brilliant smile radiating from her face. She put her left hand in front of her smile, showing off a large diamond. "Don and I went mineral hunting, you know that geology stuff".

"Oh my God!" Susan shouted with joy. "Congratulations! Don, were you going to mention this?"

Don laughed. "What are you talking about? Do you know this girl? I've never seen her before in my life!"

"Yeah, and pigs fly," Larry said clearly delighted.

Don went over and put his arm around Kathy. "Can you believe this crazy girl? She loves me."

Larry said, "There's no accounting for taste."

Susan declared, "Enough of this nonsense. I'm getting the good Champagne."

"Thanks, but before you go I have an important question? What would you think if we kick off the opening of the winery with a wedding party? My dad agreed to foot the bill."

Susan said, "I can't think of anything I'd rather do. And your dad doesn't get to pay. Mi casa es su casa."

"Wonderful!" Kathy said, dancing with excitement.

Susan asked, "When?"

Kathy looked on the calendar on the wall, "How about spring break with the grapes and the apples in bloom?"

Susan said, "Sounds perfect. This is wonderful news. Can I tell the rest of the party?"

"No way! I get to tell them. Didn't you say something about Champagne?" Laughing, Kathy ran into the living room holding out her left hand.

Larry remained in the kitchen with Don. "I'm just curious. What about the Jewish thing? Is she going to convert?"

"No, I've never been very religious. My

parents were a little concerned, but when they met Kathy, they melted. Besides it's not like they went to temple all the time. The only time they do the Jewish thing is on holidays. For now we are just taking the best of our cultures. If and when we have kids, they can choose what they want to believe."

"Do you think that will work?"

"It works for me. I'm kind of a 'Jewbu' myself."

"What's that?"

"Half Jewish, half Buddhist."

"That's so ridiculous it's funny."

Don laughed and shrugged, "It's my Karma."

Chapter 14
Southern California Blues

Alice Johnson hated USC. The student body went en masse to the Saturday football games, with cheerleaders that reminded her of the things she hated at high school. It seemed like half the students wanted to be actors, waiting to be discovered and the other half wanted to be surfer dudes or beach bunnies. University of Spoiled Children, she thought. I should have known from the nickname. And there was no way she wanted to pledge for a sorority.

She remembered coming down to LA with her

parents—the beaches, Disneyland, Hollywood. It seemed like the land of nonstop fun. She knew the fun had to stop. She didn't want to be a disco doll. Most importantly, she knew the cocaine had to stop. It made her just want it more and more, then she'd come down, strung out, with nose bleeds. She needed to stop the endless high school senior prom.

December 7, 1974, Alice awoke to the sound of her dorm-mate having sex with her boyfriend. Not again! Alice thought as the girl across the room tried to muffle her screams with a pillow. Jennifer, her bleached-blond roommate looked over and saw that she had awakened Alice. "Sorry," she said, and then her boyfriend returned to the job of giving her oral sex.

Alice ran to the bathroom in her nightie, noticing the boyfriend checking her out in spite of his busy morning activity. She showered, threw on slacks, a long-sleeved USC t-shirt, and walked out into the southern California smog-filtered sunshine. The winter rain had still not yet made an appearance. Hollywood, she remembered reading in yesterday's

Los Angeles Times, was happy with the extended sunshine. It could keep shooting films outdoors and get more reels in the can. God, she missed northern California. She went back to the dorm to the pay phone in the hall and dialed her parent's number. "Mom, I need to come home."

*

The semester ended and Bill started working part time at the VA clinic. Free from his classes, he enjoyed spending his time off with Tina. The whole household had adopted her. Summer, Laura, and Rick all took turns picking her up from school and taking her to gymnastics classes. When the December weather allowed, Auntie Laura would take Tina for a ride on Chardonnay with Tilden running alongside.

On a day off, Bill took Tina to the winery in late December to visit Don and Kathy. The three were talking and sharing a bottle of wine in the great room as Tina played with her Barbie in front of a huge window that faced the courtyard.

"So are you planning the wedding?" Bill asked his high school friend and his fiancée.

Don asked, "Will you be the best man?"

"I would consider it an honor."

Kathy asked, "How would you feel about Tina being the flower girl?"

Bill smiled. "Button, would you like that?"

"What's a flower girl?" Kathy explained, Tina smiled and asked, "Do I get a new dress?"

"Oh yes, I'll take you out for that when I get my wedding dress."

"Just like my Barbie!" Tina said, her broad smile lighting up her face like a Christmas tree.

*

After school in mid-December, Bill brought Tina to her childcare center. He knew she was getting a new after-school teacher, because Mrs. Lyndon had left for a maternity leave. Bill walked into the big multipurpose room holding hands with Tina. Alice Johnson, sitting on the floor surrounded by ten children, looked up at him. Even without makeup dressed conservatively in slacks and a blouse he could almost feel the radiance of her charisma and it took his breath away. She looked somehow familiar.

She let the other children continue to color with crayons and rose to introduce herself. "You must be Tina," she said, with a soothing voice and a welcoming smile. She turned to Bill and said, "I'm Alice, like in Wonderland. I'm Tina's new caretaker."

"You look somehow familiar. Did you go to Sonoma State?"

"We never actually met. I'm Susan and Larry's daughter. I briefly dated your roommate Rick last year."

"Oh, the Disco Queen." He regretted saying it as soon as the words spilled out of his mouth.

She blushed deeply, her cheeks matching Tina's hair. "I'm trying to put all that behind me."

"I'm sorry. I didn't mean to embarrass you."

"It's okay. I guess I was a little out of control for a while. I'm trying to change." She pointed behind her to the children. I'm going to Sonoma State, while working here part time. Going to be a teacher."

Partly from feeling guilty for humiliating her and some other reason he didn't yet understand, he said, "I'll be picking up Tina in two hours. We could take her for an ice cream together."

"Listen, I don't know what Rick told you but…"

"No, no, he interrupted. I really am sorry I said that. I just thought we could talk. I know about people trying to change. I work with Veterans. It can be hard."

She felt his sincerity. In spite of her mixed feelings she agreed, "Just ice cream."

Tina said, "Oh boy, ice cream!"

*

That night Bill told Rick about meeting Alice and enjoying her company when they went for ice cream. Rick could see he was already under her spell.

Rick said, "She was a serious user of cocaine. You certainly don't want to deal with another woman who has an addiction problem, do you?"

"She told me about that. Just got out of a rehab program. I believe she really wants to change."

"You really like the difficult cases. Don't you?"

"Not really. But there is something about her.

"Wow, you really like her."

"I believe I do. She's quite brave."

Rick smiled, "Being brave was never a problem for Alice. I hope you're right, she's got it kicked. I like her a lot."

"So you don't mind…"

"Not at all. I'm happily in love with Laura. Bill, I wanted to tell you something else."

Bill leaned forward to pay attention. "Yeah?"

"I nominated you for the Darwin Award for student of the year in the sciences and to speak at graduation. I know it's real early but you know how these things work. It goes from committee to committee then it's voted on by a student committee."

"I'm flattered. But why? There are lots of students smarter than me."

"Maybe, but your GPA is up there with the best. Your resiliency is unbelievable. After the shit that you have gone through I think I would have found a quiet place to hide. But it's not enough you're are a single parent now and still volunteer to work at the Vet Center. You even have the nerve to kick my ass at ultimate Frisbee and softball."

"Rick, I couldn't do it without you, Laura and Summer."

"Just happy to help out. I'm really fond of Tina."

"Okay, my turn. You're pretty damn impressive yourself. You started a business on your own, had your wife screw with you financial well-being, went back to school, invited us into you house, helped care for Tina. Then, you have the audacity to find the most charismatic women I've ever met, Laura, and she falls in love with you.

"I've seen a lot of officers in the military that didn't know shit but think they were hot stuff and got people killed. But Rick, I would follow you into battle any day and know you got my back."

"Bill, I've heard that men aren't supposed to talk to each other like this, just grunt once in a while."

"Sorry man, don't know what got into me. Fuck you."

"No motherfucker, fuck you."

"Okay that's better, let's get a beer and burp."

"Now you're talking."

*

For a week Bill and Alice met almost every day. She felt so comfortable with him, having someone to talk to and reveal her true self.

Bill asked Alice, "Have you even been to a Hanukkah celebration?"

"No, it's a Jewish thing right?" Alice said.

"Don and Kathy are coming over tomorrow night to light the candles with Laura and me for the eighth night of Hanukkah. Maybe you'd like to come?"

"Are you Jewish?

"Half, on my mother's side. I like to celebrate everything. It's the Winter Solstice also. I always include that."

"Will Rick be there?" Alice asked.

"Of course, he lives there and is one of my best friends."

"That might be awkward."

"Can you handle awkward?"

She smiled that wicked brave smile. "Yes, I

think I can. . . do you think Rick can?"

"Yes, I mentioned you to him. He is so in love with Laura he will barely notice you are there."

Tina eliminated her last doubts. "Please come, Alice."

"How can I say, 'no to her'?"

*

When Alice came to the Ponderosa, Rick made a point of greeting her with a hug. It was Laura who put Alice at ease, taking her in both hands, telling her she was welcome and kissing her on the cheek. Don and Kathy arrived, Laura ran and hugged her brother and soon to be sister-in-law. Laura and Don told stories about growing up together. Don recalled one story, "Remember when you were 16 and used the Hanukkah candles to burn your bra to support feminism. I thought Mom was going to kill you."

"Yeah," Laura said, laughing so hard her side hurt, "Dad had to put the fire out with a bucket of water."

Finally, when things calmed down, they all took turns lighting the Hanukkah candles.

A Christmas tree stood next to the menorah in the living room, presents stacked underneath. True to his word, Bill lit a special candle for the solstice. "We ask humbly, please Mother Nature bring back the sun." He said like he was serious, but they all knew it was all done tongue- in-cheek.

The roommates were quite comfortable in their diversity. Tina sat with her head in Summer's lap. Alice could only look with wonder at the closeness of these friends.

Chapter 15
Spring Bloom

Golden Eagle Vineyard, reborn in spring, hummed with activity. Just a week earlier vines that stood naked were budding with baby green leaves. Winter rains gave hillside grasses an emerald sheen. Orchards of apple and other fruit trees burst with flowers, exploding in color. Over a hundred people gathered for Don and Kathy's wedding in the outdoor paradise of the Dry Creek Valley.

The bride's flowing snowy-white dress contrasted with her rich tan Eurasian skin and shimmering black hair, highlighting Kathy's unique beauty. Tina wore a frozen smile and a new blue dress as she walked in front of the bride, tossing ruby red rose pedals that matched her braided hair. Don and Laura's mother Sylvia lit a candle and said the magic Hebrew words of their ancestors. The Buddhist monk from Kathy's mother's Korean temple officiated and married the young couple.

Laura, the maid of honor looked stunning in her Tahoe blue gown flowing to the floor but slit on one side showing off one long lovely leg.

Bill, the best man, was dressed in a wide-lapel tuxedo and frilly white shirt, somehow popular in the early seventies. Alice Johnson accompanied him. They continued to meet often after Tina's child care. Bill tried not to stare at his date. She had always dressed so conservatively at daycare. Now he saw her decked out in a short creamy dress, her blonde hair curled into little ringlets. God, she's fuckin' gorgeous, he thought.

The reception in the garden included two hundred people eating and drinking as the band played popular rock n' roll. The group, members of the geology department, made up for a lack of talent with a lot of enthusiasm. As the afternoon turned into evening, Summer volunteered to take Tina home, leaving Bill free to complete his duties as best man.

He checked to make sure the limo would be there at midnight to take the couple to the airport hotel before their early morning flight to Paris. The couple's honeymoon to France included the always romantic City of Lights and touring the lovely wine-soaked Bordeaux countryside with beautiful castles and hillsides. They would be gone during the two-week spring break.

The party continued into the evening. There were three kegs, one filled with beer. The other two contained wine, white and red, the quality quite good, from a neighboring winery. Marijuana smoke filled the air as the band played well into the night.

As the clock neared midnight the limo arrived. Final toasts to the newlyweds were led by Bill, who by that time was starting to slur his words. Don insisted that Bill not drive home in his condition.

He told him to sleep it off in his empty room. Bill agreed knowing Alice had her own room in her parent's home. When the couple departed in the limo, Bill stumbled into Don's room and immediately fell asleep.

He dreamed of Alice and imagined that she was an award-winning Cabernet. He inhaled her bouquet, savored her flavor, and drank deeply, his glass never empty until he was drunk and swooning. The drink filled the emptiness he felt in his heart. It had disappeared that night, at least for one glorious dream.

Bill awoke in the morning without a hangover. Eyes still closed he smiled remembering the dream. His nose filled with her lovely scent. Was he still dreaming? His eyes opened and she lay next to him, cuddled in his arms, almost purring like a kitten. Oh my God--it wasn't a dream. She came to him last night. She still slept, eyes closed, face angelic. He watched her and felt tears of joy run down his face.

Her eyes finally opened, so blue and clear like two crystal pools of water. He wanted to dive in and lose himself in those deep turquoise pools. Instead he looked fondly at her.

"I think I'm in love with you," she whispered.

He kissed her lightly, tenderly as if he were afraid the spell would break if he touched too hard. He explored every part of her this time with his eyes wide open, awash in her radiance. Their bodies danced together in some tantalizing ballet until they were satiated, sore, spent. A final kiss sealed their love.

"You are incredible," he said.

"I didn't know I was until now. Sex was always just for fun, part of an act. This time I felt like I was part of you."

"I love you too Alice, so much. But I have a daughter now. I have to be sure…"

"Oh, it's a package deal?"

"Yes."

"Good. I think one of the reasons I'm in love with you is Tina.

"It's spring break, let's take her to Disneyland. I've never been."

"Really…You want to go to L.A.?" She had just left that city behind. She hated being there. Then she thought about going to Disneyland with her parents when she was Tina's age. Warmth ran through her body. "Yes," She heard herself saying, "I'd love to go there with you and Tina."

Chapter 16
Summer's Secret

There was a part of Summer she had not shared with anyone. She had never liked dating in high school, but was popular and went on her fair share of dates. Prom night proved a huge disappointment. Tom, her date, dressed in his tux did look cute. Her friend Becky told her she was so lucky, "He's a total catch."

She felt elegant in her black velour floor length dress, low cut, off the shoulder. He danced well and the local rock band played all the right music. So why did it feel wrong? After the date Tom was all over her in the backseat of the car, his hands pawing under her bra and under her dress. She gave him a quick hand job and felt disgusted. Tom smiled stupidly, satisfied and took her home. He moved in for the goodnight kiss but she flew out the door. "Goodnight," she called half-way up the steps to her house.

Her first year in college, she lost her virginity to John Thompson on their second date. He came less than a minute after putting on the Trojan, leaving her unsatisfied, unfulfilled, and unhappy. That date would be their last. Summer had fun with boys until they wanted to have sex, then she lost interest. Am I frigid, she wondered?

She both loved and envied Laura, Kathy and Alice. They were so beautiful and comfortable with their sexuality. She started having fantasies about each of them and found the idea exciting. Could she be a lesbian? Just the word gave her the creeps. Her parents—father Irish, mother Mexican—revered the Catholic Church. Putting the inkling of homosexuality out of her mind she refused to approach the very idea. SHE WAS NOT GAY.

Her world was about to be turned upside down. Spring break was almost over, Alice, Bill, and Tina returned from their LA trip, the two adults obviously in love. Auntie Summer spent the day with Tina, babysitting. She loved the time she spent with the girl. In the afternoon, Bill came home to the Ponderosa, car filled with groceries. "Summer, I'm back if you want to go out."

"I think I will, just to go get a beer and get out of the house." She kissed him on the cheek, went into her room, put on a white blouse which she tucked into a clean pair of jeans and decided to drive to downtown Petaluma, just to go somewhere different away from the college crowd. She found a bar open by the river and walked in, showed the bartender her fake ID and ordered a Bohemia beer. She heard someone pull up in a Harley and cut the engine. When Suzanne Langston walked into the bar Summer couldn't take her eyes off her. Skintight leather pants hugged her bottom, a silver chain looped loosely as a belt. Her red leather jacket covered a frilly black silk top encasing her ample breasts. The leather clad woman's long reddish-brown locks were set free after she took off her helmet and shook her head.

Suzanne returned Summer's stare with a smile. Her bright green eyes shined in the bar door's back-light. She took the stool next to Summer and told the bartender, "That looks good. I'll have what she's having." Turning to Summer, "My name is Suzanne, I've never seen you in here before."

"Never been in here before. I live up in Penngrove. I'm a student at Sonoma State. My name is Summer." Electricity ran through her body as she felt the woman's firm handshake.

"So you slumming it down here?"

"Just thought I'd try someplace different. That's quite an outfit you have on. For your motorcycle, I guess."

"Yeah, but to tell you the truth," and she leaned forward showing the younger woman her cleavage and whispered in the Summer's ear, "I like the feel of leather on my skin."

Summer felt goose-bumps moving down her skin. Words eluded her. Finally she asked, "So what do you do for a living?"

"If you can guess, I'll give you a ride."

"I have no clue. Secretary?"

"Try again."

"Give me a hint."

"Ok, I graduated from UC Berkeley."

"Really, wow, okay, chemist?"

"No, give up?"

"Okay, what?"

"I teach second grade in San Rafael."

Summer's jaw dropped. "You don't look like my second grade teacher."

"I'll take that as a compliment. Go ahead and finish your beer. I'll take you for a ride anyway. The road out to Bodega Bay is awesome. You should see it on the back of a Harley."

Outside in the evening sunlight Suzanne handed Summer a helmet, kick-started the bike and told her to hang on tight. They soared along the country road out to the bay and Summer learned to lean on each curve holding tight almost like dancing. The two women quietly watched the sunset over the bay.

"I can't believe you teach second grade and ride a Harley."

"Hey, I love teaching and my students, but they don't need to know what Ms. Langston does when she gets home to Petaluma. Listen, can I kiss you?"

Shock hit Summer like a slap in the face. "I. . . I don't know. I've never been kissed by a woman before." Suzanne leaned in and lightly brushed her lips against the younger woman's mouth. Summer felt tingles down to her toes.

"Come on sweet-cakes, let's go back to my place." Summer didn't answer. She just climbed on behind Ms. Langston and held onto her through all the curves on the road.

Back at the second grade teacher's little house on D Street, Suzanne unzipped and tantalizingly stripped off her leather pants. She had nothing on underneath, revealing light red pubic hair shaved in the shape of a heart. Summer watched, unable to move forward or retreat. Naked, Suzanne pulled off Summer's clothing. The host took control, her fingers dancing along the younger girl's body. Lips found lips, breasts spilled together, and the teacher found her student's nectar. Summer opened like a flower in bloom, surrendering. She screamed with the orgasm that she had waited her whole life to feel. After the passion, Summer cried, her sexuality undeniable.

The older woman kissed her tears. "It's okay baby," and she held her in tight embrace.

*

Summer sat with Laura in the living room at the Ponderosa, having just explained her revelation. "How in the world am I going to tell my parents?"

Laura asked, "How would your parents deal with this?"

"Are you kidding? No wedding, no kids. I'm a damn homo! I can't even deal with it."

"What does Suzanne say? How does she deal with it?"

"It's like a secret life, the straight teacher, the

gay leather-bound biker."

"So you could stay in the closet."

"Laura, I don't know what to do."

"Well, Summer, I love you, Tina loves you. Do you think Bill, Alice, or Rick will love you any less? They don't give a shit who you choose to have sex with."

"Should I tell them?"

"I would. Those guys were always there for me, especially after the… the rape."

"I know, I love them like brothers."

"Summer, are you going to see her again?"

"God, I hope so."

"Can I watch?" Laura teased.

"Shut the fuck up, bitch." Summer laughed with Laura in spite of everything.

Laura said, "Summer, this is all going to work out. Think of Bill, he had to deal with Vietnam and Lisa. I had to deal with being raped. You can deal with this. You could always move to Berkeley. You would fit right in."

"I'm not moving to Berkeley. If I am gay,

here's as good a place as any. Laura thanks. I love you so much."

"Sorry, I'm seeing someone." They laughed again.

Chapter 17
The End of an Era

In the late spring of 1975 a For Sale sign appeared at the front of the driveway to the Penngrove Ponderosa. Rick and his Ponderosa family were moving out. Rick, on track to graduate with his BS degree was moving north to Dry Creek, to his new house on the grounds of the Golden Eagle Vineyards and Winery, with his new decorator and lover, Laura. Chardonnay already grazed on a hillside pasture.

Rick had noticed a difference in Laura since they had professed their love. Still possessing her wicked sense of humor, she became more centered. She found a new sense of purpose. Having finished her course work in January, she joined Bill in working full time at the Veteran's Center. The last paragraphs were almost completed on her master's thesis.

One class separated Bill from his nursing psych designation to add to his degree as an RN. Rick couldn't believe his good friend and Alice were together. Her transformation defied his imagination. Gone was the Disco Queen he had dated. Alice thrived in her role as Tina's unofficial mother. She signed up for classes at Sonoma as an education major, determined to become an elementary school teacher. This pseudo-family found a house in South Santa Rosa. Tilden somehow sensed the move and every time Bill left the house he stood looking longingly at the door until his master returned. Summer, still a full time student, would be their part time nanny and house-mate.

Summer came out to them in a house meeting, out to only them. For now she was staying in the closet to everyone else. Bill laughed when she told them. "I had a feeling," he said.

"Bull shit," Laura called. "You didn't know didley."

"Really, something told me."

"Okay," Laura relented, "can we get back to Summer's story now?"

"Sorry," Bill said. "Still I had a feeling."

They all laughed.

Each of them hugged Summer after her confession. Relieved, tears still streamed down her face. "You are the best friends a person could have."

Laura teased, "Ready to tell your parents?"

"Hell no!" and the tears turned to laughter.

*

Graduation day at Sonoma State University started foggy and cold. The marine layer invaded from the west like the guy who always shows up at the party uninvited. By late morning it was driven away by the sun. The field in front of the classroom buildings exploded in green. The college trees were still too young to dominate the buildings but the leaves still waved impressively in the breeze. The crowd gathered and proclaimed it "not too hot or too cold, great weather."

Sonoma State in the seventies did not have a valedictorian; in line with the alternative nature of the school where some teachers didn't even give grades, just pass or fail.

So the faculty, administration and student committees voted for their student speaker. They picked William "Bill Silver, Veteran, volunteer worker at the Vet Center and 3.8 grade point average nursing student graduate." Few in that crowd would remember the commencement speaker but no one would forget Bill.

When he took the stage he stripped off his cap and gown. The crowd gasped, then stood and cheered. Underneath he had on his dress white navy uniform complete with a chest full of medals. He started:

"I wore this uniform, for better or worse, for three long years. I am not standing before you in this outfit because of pride or to show my support for the Vietnam War. I am wearing it for the memories of many of my friends and all the others who died or were wounded in body or mind during that incursion. I watched in horror last month as the American government flew the last helicopters out of Saigon as people who supported us were left behind. The leaders who sent us there should hide their faces in shame."

He turned for a second to the congressman sitting on the platform who had voted to send troops to the war. The House member turned red and looked away. "Good men were sent to risk life or limb in that war for what? I think they said something about dominoes. Well Vietnam fell and the rest of the dominoes are still standing.

"The strategy of that war was poorly planned, was fought for the wrong reasons and we left the place like rats securing out of a kitchen when the lights are turned on. Someone please go to Kissinger and take his Nobel Peace Prize back. One of my best friends was killed there. I am now the father of his child. When you people vote in the future, make damn sure you don't vote for a war unless there is a

Hitler threatening the whole world or some invasion force is off the shores of this country. Thank you."

The students and their guests gave him a standing ovation. "Follow that," he said to the congressman who was due to speak next.

*

The ranch house stood empty and naked. The papers signed. Laura and Rick were the lasts ones out.

"Say goodbye to the Penngrove Ponderosa," Rick said with a slight tugging on his heart strings.

"I can't say goodbye to something that does not exist. It's no longer the Ponderosa. You signed the papers, it's no longer yours. No Rick Cartwright, no Ponderosa."

He laughed. "I guess even the best TV shows go off the air."

"Yup, even the best," Laura agreed.

Rick turned off the light and shut the door.

Other books by Nathaniel Robert Winters:

Rumors about my Father and Other Stories

A Memoir-Novella

This was my first book written after my father's death: follows his life through prohibition, The Depression and World War II

The Legend of Heath Angelo

A Memoir-Novella

I met Heath in 1977 at the Nature Conservancy Preserve he created in Mendocino County.

Finding Shelter from the Cold

A Young Adult novel that makes a book for dog lovers of all ages.

No Place for a Wallflower

Iola Hitt's Letters of the Second World War

A Memoir-Novella

Iola was a young 93 when I met her and wrote about her involvement during World War II.

The Adventures of the Omaha Kid

A Novel of Sports, Romance and the Search for Love

About the Author

Nathaniel Robert Winters was born in Brooklyn in 1950 and grew up mostly in Valley Stream, New York a suburban town on Long Island. After serving a tour of duty in the Navy he fell in love with Northern California and made the area his home. He graduated from Sonoma State University and achieved a Master's in Education from California State University Stanislaus. He enjoyed the opportunity to be a high school history and science teacher for the Turlock School District for 33 years. For many years an avid skier and tennis player, he also coached baseball and soccer. He currently lives in Saint Helena, a small town in the wine-growing region of Napa Valley with his wife, son and dog. Bob has an affinity for nature and loves to travel. His family has hosted foreign exchange students from France, the Czech Republic and Russia. He has been diagnosed with Parkinson's disease and still writes almost every day.

Made in the USA
Charleston, SC
30 August 2014